LOVE'S EVIDENCE

LOVE'S
EVIDENCE

•

Jeanette Sparks

AVALON BOOKS
NEW YORK

PRINTED IN THE UNITED STATES OF AMERICA
ON ACID-FREE PAPER
BY HADDON CRAFTSMEN, BLOOMSBURG, PENNSYLVANIA

With loving and heartfelt memories,
this book is dedicated to my son, Kurt.

Chapter One

Night fell like a theater curtain over the Port of Miami. Nate Mansfield stared out at the surrounding buildings as lights flickered on. The stakeout had been successfully completed and he breathed a sigh of relief. All the tenants were still out of the apartment and he wanted to keep it that way until last-minute police work was completed. A stinging wind hit the back of his neck. He pulled his jacket closer over the bulky bulletproof vest, wishing it wasn't regulation.

Just when he thought everything was in order, a woman appeared from around the corner of a building, causing a tidal wave of attention. The area supposedly had been cordoned off. His walkie-talkie signaled.

"What's going on? How did that dame get through the barrier?" Nate's captain barked. "Get her out of there—fast."

Oblivious to what was taking place, the woman climbed the steps to the apartment entrance. She held

1

a sack of groceries on her hip and fished for a key in her purse.

Nate dropped the walkie-talkie in his pocket and took off across the street. His heels thumped on the oil-stained asphalt. He leaped up the steps. Seeing the fright in her eyes, he was about to explain that he was a policeman, when she wrenched back, dropping the sack. A jar of mayonnaise shattered on the cement, oozing its milky-white contents on the steps.

Nate grabbed her before she fell, muffling her scream with the palm of his hand. With terror-filled eyes, she fought vainly to free herself, giving him a sharp whack in the ribs with an elbow. He grunted.

Catching his breath, he pinned her arms before she could do more damage. "It's okay, lady. I'm a cop."

She glanced at his blue jeans. "No way, buddy. Now let me go!"

He released her, and drew out his badge. "Sorry about the misunderstanding, but I really am a policeman."

Nate helped her pick up the sack and retrieve the groceries. He could tell she was angry by the set of her mouth. When he got a better look at her under the light, he broke into a broad grin.

"Kitty? Kitty O'Hara?"

"Nate?"

"By heavens, it is you!" He stood grinning at her. "This is unbelievable. Just great!"

Kitty blinked. "I think I'm dreaming," she said, not sure whether she should be glad or furious.

Nate, the boy who lived next door when she was growing up, had been transformed into a tall, good-looking, broad-chested man. His eyes showed quick intelligence, and he still had that nice smile.

She felt her face flush. "What's going on here? You scared me half to death."

"You wouldn't want to know. Police stuff."

"Then I'm glad I was away shopping." She sensed the change in him. He was not a man to be taken lightly. "My heart's still beating too fast. I thought you were a mugger."

"Have you lived in this neighborhood long?" He scratched his jaw, as though surprised she'd live in such a place.

"Make it past tense. This was all a big mistake. I'm moving out of here just as quickly as I can." She didn't add that the rent was dirt cheap for the two rooms or that she was trying to break into the cosmetics business on a shoestring. "I'm trying to get out of here. But Miami rents are staggering and I haven't landed a job yet." She stopped, and her hand flew to her mouth. "Oh, gosh! Does that make me a vagrant?"

Nate grinned. "Not really." His tone offered a soft apology. "You were about to walk in on a crime scene." He whipped out a legal form from his pocket. "Sorry to trouble you, but I'll need a statement."

"From me? Why? I wasn't even here."

His eyes, blue reservoirs, were direct. "We're getting statements from everyone who lives in the building."

"Right now?"

"Now's a good time unless you prefer to come to the station in the morning. Here, let me set your groceries inside the door."

Kitty handed him the key and he inserted it in the lock. She didn't like his official stance. Although she kept outwardly calm, inside she was shaking with a mixture of surprise, resentment, and curiosity. "I guess

I'd rather do it right here. I've got an interview to-morrow."

He pointed down the street. "There's a café halfway down the block. Let's go get a cup of coffee."

Kitty felt a little less resentful. At least he was being civilized about it and not expecting her to stand under the streetlight. He called to another officer, his voice deep and commanding, and said he'd check in later. Then he took her arm and they fell into step.

Nate held the door open for Kitty at the café. The run-down place had only a few booths along a wall opposite the counter. Stale food odors and grease hung in the air. They slid into a black vinyl booth, facing each other.

Nate took a quick look at his wristwatch. Dark circles were etched under his eyes. "Past dinnertime and I'm starved. Let's order hamburgers as long as we're here."

Kitty had her doubts about whether the kitchen would rate an A, but it was too late now. "Okay."

Nate smiled. "Real good to see you, Kitty."

"Small world." She was beginning to feel more like herself, conscious of his gaze on her. She waited for him to speak, wanting to hear the familiar sound of his voice. It had mellowed with the years.

A middle-aged waitress in stained flats sidled up to take their orders. When Kitty asked for a veggie burger, the woman raised her penciled brows and frowned, shaking her head. "You gotta' be kiddin', honey."

Nate's eyes crinkled with good humor.

"Make it a plain burger, but hold the onions, please," Kitty said, corralling her annoyance. Nate ordered everything on his.

When the waitress moved away, he put on his official face again, took out a form, and laid it on the scarred table, a pen poised in his big hand. "Let's get this over with. How long have you lived in that apartment building?"

"Just a month."

"Did you know the men in the next apartment?"

She shook her head. "I didn't know anyone. Surely you don't think for one minute that I—"

Before she finished her sentence, his next question came, rapid-fire, followed by several more. And he never once smiled. Kitty felt unnerved under his scrutiny and kept saying no to his probing.

Finally he put the form in the inside pocket of his jacket and relaxed. She caught a glimpse of a holster under his arm, and tried to imagine him with a suspect in an interrogation room.

"That's about all I need to ask you for now," he said.

"For now? I don't understand. Why would you ask me more? I don't know anything else."

His mouth turned up in a smile. "You indicated you'd probably be moving soon. Let me know where you decide to settle. Got another place picked out?" He handed her a business card.

She took the card, glanced at it, and dropped it in her purse. Then she let her breath out in a long sigh.

"It's only tentative," she said, "and probably more than I can afford. But I'll give you a call when I know for sure."

Nate glanced toward the door and Kitty managed a corner-of-an-eye glimpse at his profile. Two scruffy men came in, baseball caps turned backward. In gruff voices they ordered coffee at the counter. They eyed Kitty, then huddled together, talking in hushed tones.

Outside the café window, it was dark, except for the garish reflection of a red-and-green neon sign. With all that had happened, Kitty was glad she wasn't alone, and had no doubt Nate could take care of her if push came to shove.

The waitress brought the hamburgers, along with mugs of strong black coffee. Kitty picked up the burger, feeling awkward in his presence, something she had never experienced when they were kids.

"Smells good," he said, and used both hands to pick up his half-pound monster. "Dig in."

Kitty's stomach growled and she took a bite. She was hungrier than she thought. The burger might be a cholesterol time bomb, but it was delicious.

Nate felt jazzed sitting there across from Kitty. She'd always had a way of making him feel good. He watched her with growing interest as she took a sip of coffee, her upper lip delicately covering a portion of the rim. She was far more than pretty now—beautiful would better describe her. Her chin-length hair was that same deep coppery color he'd always admired. The curiosity in those primrose-blue eyes staring back at him nearly took his breath away.

He wiped his mouth on a paper napkin. "I haven't seen you in what—ten years?"

"Something like that. You seldom wrote after you went off to college."

"Shame on me—you being the prettiest gal at Palmella High School. I'll bet you didn't pine very long, though." He grinned.

She didn't quite look him in the eye. "I didn't pine for you at all," she said.

"Married?"

"No. You?"

Her breathy voice did something to him. "Came close once, but never found anyone who'd have me."

She chuckled. It sounded like music. "I'll bet."

The texture of her lips made him think of rose petals, and he wondered what they would feel like if he kissed them. Then he told himself he was thinking insane thoughts. He wasn't even sure who she was now after all this time.

Still, his thoughts went right on rolling like a movie screen. Then he said right out of the blue, "Kitty, it'd be a crime if you don't get to know me again."

She struggled to suppress a smile. "You're pretty sure of yourself, Nate Mansfield."

He laughed. "Promise you won't forget to stay in touch."

She nodded. "If you bring me here for another burger."

He grinned. "You bet. Name the day."

She didn't reply.

When they finished eating, he paid the bill and walked Kitty back to her apartment, hesitant about leaving her there alone, even though the crisis was over. Someone had wiped away the mayonnaise. He picked up the sack inside the door and handed it to her, wondering how she had ended up in this fleabag.

After they parted, Nate settled in behind the steering wheel of his car. He could still hear the music of her voice in his ears. The memory of her smile lingered in his mind and he traced a pattern on the steering wheel before turning on the ignition and driving down the inky black street.

Later that night, Nate lay awake, his heart beating like a drum as the memories of Kitty O'Hara flooded back. He'd worked hard to forget her after he graduated from high school. She had been adamantly opposed to his going into law enforcement. It was the one thing he wanted to do with his life. Her father, a state trooper, had been gunned down in the line of duty when Kitty was about twelve. She never got over it.

For most of their young lives they had lived next door to each other as good friends. Now Kitty was back—beautiful, sleek, and every inch a desirable woman.

Nate liked being a cop. He had a good track record, although he never worked at promoting himself. What made him feel good was being able to keep up the pace. What would Kitty feel about his work now?

A sudden memory of a moonlit night surfaced as though it were only yesterday. He and Kitty didn't go straight home after the Christmas formal dance. They drove down a rutted dirt road near the lake and he kissed her. He could almost taste her creamy lips even now.

He grinned at the recollection, a lump in his throat. But that was a different time, light-years away. He knew he couldn't bring back the past. Still, the two of them had a history.

He rubbed the stubble on his jaw. She still dazzled him just as she had when they were teenagers. Now, by some strange fluke, they had been hauled back into each other's lives.

* * *

Kitty lay on her back, sleepless, listening to the sounds of the night. A rafter creaked, a night bird called, a frog in the overgrown shrubs outside the window croaked. In the distance a foghorn groaned like an eerie voice from another world.

She thought about her encounter with Nate Mansfield with amused resignation. He had really frightened her when he grabbed her at the door of the apartment building. She would probably never see him again. But he had given her his card. Nate—a cop. Something told her he had developed into a smart, tough, slightly egocentric man. But did he still have his tender side?

Scenes from the past bounced around in her head in little vignettes. Amazingly, a stirring of nostalgia crept over her, bringing on an involuntary smile. She remembered when he first kissed her up in the tree house behind his home when she was twelve. Their teeth had scraped. It was awful.

She sighed, and glanced at the telephone beside the bed. If he didn't call her, would she have the courage to call him?

Chapter Two

Kitty got a call from Nate the next night. Excited, she tried to form casual sentences, but ran them together too fast.

"Everything okay?" he asked.

"Just fine."

He still had that same charismatic quality in his voice. Her desire to see him created an excitement deep inside her that left her feeling slightly guilty. After all, she was seeing Rick Grant these days. But why should she feel guilty about wanting to stay in contact with an old friend?

"It takes me back, just to hear you speak," he said.

"It's been a long time."

"How about going out for coffee? I didn't know I was getting the night off or I'd have called earlier."

"That would be nice. I can be ready in about twenty minutes, if that's okay?"

"Swell. See you then."

She hung up. What would they talk about? You could only discuss old times for so long before it became boring. Did he still like sports? That topic was safe enough.

Nate picked up Kitty in his Jeep Wrangler. She was thrilled to see him. He drove a few miles down the freeway, then turned off and parked beside a neighborhood cafe. Inside, the room was furnished in emerald green, with old pictures of racehorses from the Hialeah track. Nate spoke to several people and Kitty saw right away that this was a place frequented by cops. Somehow she felt right at home.

He seated her at a corner table in a maple captain's chair then excused himself to cross the floor and speak to a couple near the kitchen. He was a totally masculine man, slender-hipped and powerfully built through the chest. He would probably dominate most situations, she suspected. Glancing around, she noted the place was only half full. Most of the patrons clustered in small groups, talking.

Nate came back and took a seat opposite. "Sorry. Had to have a word with the rookies." He relaxed. "Did I tell you how pretty you look tonight?"

Kitty rewarded him with a smile. "Thanks." Then the waitress brought back their order of coffee and apple pie. She took a sip. It tasted hot. "Mmm—good."

"Where do we start?" He leaned forward. "I want you to fill me in on all the missing pieces of your life since I saw you last."

"Whoa! That's a sizable undertaking." Her thoughts were like a traffic jam in her head as she spilled out what had happened. "After I graduated from college, I went to work in a beauty shop in Tallahassee."

"Why not your mother's shop in Palmella?" His open face glowed with vitality.

"I needed to get out of there. My reasons for keeping my hand in the business will probably bore you."

"You could never bore me. Go on."

"I needed to know what new things women were looking for. You see, I've started a cosmetics business. Remember how Mom and I used to make a lot of our own stuff in the back room of her beauty shop?"

"Sort of. That wasn't exactly a guy thing."

She flashed him an enthusiastic smile. "Things are looking up. I found a job this morning in a glitzy beauty salon in one of the big tourist hotels—and none too soon. Eventually, I hope to talk the manager into selling my line. They're really very good, if I do say so myself."

"I'm sure they are. Good luck."

"I won't tell you about my first interview at another salon downtown, though. It was too awful. The guy was a lecher, and he wore the worst-fitting toupee! I came close to relieving him of it and tossing it in his oversized lap."

"You should have confiscated it. Tell me more," he said with a straight face. "I'll go arrest the creep for harassment!"

She laughed. He grinned back at her, revealing the last vestiges of his boyhood dimples.

"I like Miami, except for that terrible neighborhood I live in. Saving money, you know. Foolish of me."

"You got that right."

"I was living in Tallahassee until recently. The capital's great, but I needed to settle in a more cosmopolitan city in order to make the right business connections."

Nate nodded. His muscular chest expanded under his shirt, causing curly golden chest hairs to peek out above his top button. Her heart skipped a beat. It took a moment before she could remind herself she was practically engaged to Rick.

"I've missed you," Nate said. "And I've been thinking all day about when we were kids." He took a bite of the pie and swallowed a sip of coffee. "Remember when you tied me to a tree down by the swamp? We'd been playing cowboys and Indians. When it got near suppertime, you took off, leaving me strung up to that darn tree. My folks had the whole neighborhood out searching. When you told my mom where we'd been playing—failing to mention you'd tied me up—she got hysterical, convinced a 'gator got her boy." He laughed at the recollection. "Palmella was a great town to grow up in."

"I remember that incident all too well. Talk about embarrassed!" Kitty said. "I was sure my mom would tan my hide, but she didn't. I guess she realized how badly I felt. But don't tell me you're still holding that against me?"

Nate reached across the table and took her hand, wrapping it gently in his own. His eyes swept casually over her face. "I would forgive you anything." He released his grip. "Kitty, I want to see you again—and soon."

She lapsed into silence. The touch of his skin and the warm intensity of his words surprised her. She was about to lay it all out, be honest regarding her relationship with Rick, when she glanced up to see a man approaching. He gave her a grin as wide as a slice of watermelon. His eyes were close-set.

"Nate, introduce me, ol' pal," the man said. He

came around Nate's shoulder and held out his brawny hand.

"You! Okay. This is my friend, Kitty O'Hara. Kitty—Jack. We work together."

Kitty said hi. She was amused by the annoyed expression on Nate's face. Jack and Nate exchanged a few affable words, then Jack politely walked away.

Nate turned his full attention back to Kitty. Why did his gaze make her draw in her breath like a schoolgirl? "You said you'd like to see me again," she said. "I think that would be nice—since we're old friends. But I have to be honest with you. I have someone in my life right now."

"Serious?"

She nodded. "His name's Rick Grant. He's interning here at Miami General. He'll be finished in a few months. We've talked about getting married after he's in practice."

Nate arched his ginger-colored brows, his strong angular face unsmiling. "Only talked about it? I don't see a ring."

Kitty scrunched her nose, hoping her freckles weren't doing a little jig. "Rick spends most of his time at the hospital. When he isn't there, he's studying. In all honesty, I don't see as much of him as I'd like to. But, fortunately, it won't be much longer."

Nate didn't reply. He leaned forward, touched her wrist, and studied her for a moment. "I just want to see you—be your friend again. No strings attached."

Kitty breathed easier. She refused to ask herself why the touch of his hand caused this fluttery feeling in the pit of her stomach.

"You told me the other evening you're not married,

Nate, but you must see someone on a regular basis—an attractive man like you. What's her name?"

"That's water under the bridge." His jaw tightened, and his look conveyed to her in no uncertain terms that he didn't want to discuss it.

When they finished the coffee refill, they got up and strolled outside. Kitty shivered. The weather had turned cooler than usual and she kicked herself for not bringing along a sweater. The ivory rayon dress she wore didn't offer much warmth. Her first inclination was to grab Nate's arm and snuggle close, but discretion held her back. This was a man she really didn't know any longer.

Nate gave her his jacket. Kitty was nearly a head shorter than him. He breathed in her scent. She'd developed a style uniquely her own, and already he was slightly nuts about her. Her figure curved flatteringly in all the right places. He could sense there was something charged about the air between them, written in every glance they'd shared in the cafe. But he resolved to keep his feelings under wraps—at least for now, not wanting to crowd her.

He opened the door of his Jeep Wrangler and she slid in. His heart did a double beat as he came around and got in beside her.

She tossed him a smile that made his heart race.

"I thought after you were in college for awhile you might decide not to go into law enforcement," she said.

They were almost back to her place. "Maybe it runs in the family. My dad was the sheriff, remember? But no, I never considered *not* doing it for a moment."

"Before yesterday, I couldn't picture you apprehending a thief, or worse, chasing a murderer. But there you were, putting your life on the line. You must court danger every time you go to work." The very thought caused her insides to churn.

"You make it sound awfully melodramatic. Most of the time I'm just investigating things. It can be dull."

"You're an undercover cop, right?"

"Right, a cop in blue jeans."

"I remember you as a pretty nice guy but full of mischief, too. Are you still the same?"

"You'll have to discover that for yourself."

Kitty pushed back a tendril of hair, speculating. Somehow she sensed a toughness about Nate. He wouldn't be a man easily crossed.

"Warm enough now, Kitty?" he asked.

"Oh, very. Here." She handed him back his jacket. "Thanks."

The following morning, the telephone's ring awakened Kitty from another nightmare, something occurring more often. She yanked the receiver off its cradle, thinking it must be Nate. "Hello," she said in an eager voice.

"It's me—Rick. I'm finally getting some time off. We'll be able to spend Christmas together. Isn't that great?"

For the first time Kitty felt mixed emotions. "Yes, of course. Do you still want to go down to my mom's in Palmella?"

"That's the plan. I'll bring my tux for the dance."

Rick went on a few more minutes, talking about how he was continuing to work those ridiculously long hours. "Let's go to a show on Friday. Okay? You pick it. I need a diversion from all this."

They met the following Friday and saw "I Love

You, Don't Touch Me," a comedy about a woman who didn't realize she was in love with her best friend, a simple sort of guy. Rick fell asleep before Kurt Valore's final romantic love song. She had awakened Rick when the credits were being shown.

Kitty and her mother, Mary, turned down a street in an exclusive Miami neighborhood looking for Mrs. Olivia Christenson's home. The expensive houses backed up to a sparkling stretch of white sandy beach.

Kitty cocked her head at her mother. "I don't know quite what to make of this. The room can't be on this street."

"The ad did say Azure Avenue, and we're on Azure now." Mary adjusted her oversized sunglasses, rubbernecking. "I don't care if it's a broom closet. You're not going back to that awful apartment house. I just cringe, thinking about you staying there. Why didn't you let me know it was in such a bad neighborhood? I'd have put my foot down in a wink."

Kitty, at twenty-six, hadn't thought it necessary to get approval, but she kept quiet.

"Over there," Mary indicated. "That's it—1706 Azure Avenue. My! It's as big as the old hotel in Palmella, don't you think, dear?"

Kitty agreed. With trepidation, she pulled her ruby-red secondhand BMW into the driveway of the large Mediterranean-style house. It was partly hidden behind a high stucco wall and coconut palms. She climbed out and adjusted her ankle-length skirt and matching blue tunic.

"Wish me luck, Mom." They strode to an ornate wrought-iron gate with a bronze metal porpoise in the center. Kitty pulled back on the squeaking hinges and let her mother pass through. Inside the courtyard a blue-tiled Moorish fountain splashed tranquil water into a tiled pond. On closer inspection Kitty noted the goldfish were plastic. The aroma of tropical plants mingled deliciously with the salty smell of the ocean. She breathed in deeply, wanting to clear her head.

With more self-confidence than she felt, she knocked on a carved door. The knock echoed from inside, as hollow as a tomb. Only a step behind her, Mary's face set in that smile she reserved for the ladies who came to her beauty shop in Palmella.

When no one answered, she said, "Maybe the newspaper printed the wrong address, after all."

Kitty gazed up at the shuttered windows on the second story. The house had that closed-up look, like a summer place used only for vacations. She shrugged, and was about to turn away, when the door opened a crack. An elderly woman peered around it. She opened the door wider and extended a thin hand with chipped fingernail polish. "Hello."

"Hi," Kitty said pleasantly. "My name's Kitty O'Hara, and . . ."

The woman brightened. "So glad you could come."

Kitty dipped her chin toward her mother. "This is Mary, my mom. We've come about a room."

The elderly woman nodded vaguely and they shook her veined hand. Kitty thought she must be the housekeeper. Ill at ease, Kitty straightened to her full five feet six inches. Her mother frowned.

"Maybe I've made a mistake," Kitty said. "I understood there was a room for rent here." The woman had hardly spoken. Kitty started to make light of the probable error, then thought better of it. "Mrs. Christenson does live here, doesn't she?"

"Oh yes, dear. There's certainly no mistake. I'm Olivia Christenson." She smiled. "Come in, won't you? We'll chat in the library."

Kitty and her mother exchanged hurried glances. With an unusually springy gait for her age, the woman led them down a wide, breezy hallway covered with Portuguese limestone. They entered a handsome room with volumes of leather-bound books in floor-to-ceiling bookcases flanking the fireplace. Mrs. Christenson crossed the room and opened French doors that led to a covered terrace with a flower garden beyond. The air that came wafting through was softly fragrant.

"Won't you sit down?" Mrs. Christenson said. Her pale blue eyes examined them with open curiosity. "Don't mind the dust. My cleaning lady didn't make it in today."

They took seats on the green-and-white striped couch that had an ivy print meandering through it. Their hostess sat down in a wingback chair across from them and offered refreshments.

Kitty did a quick take of the room's Impressionist paintings and coffered ceiling. The house reminded her of the home magazines her mother kept at the beauty shop. But she didn't miss a large spider and its intricate web in a far corner. The house, though beautiful, had unkempt look about it.

Mary spoke up, getting right down to business in her no-nonsense fashion. "May I ask what you're asking for the room?"

"It will be reasonable. I'm a widow, you see." Mrs. Christenson sighed deeply. "Hubert, my husband, was a lawyer—a brilliant New York lawyer." Her voice trailed into silence, but she perked up almost immediately, turning to Kitty. "You and I talked briefly on the telephone a few days ago."

Kitty nodded. "Right. I'll be starting a new job, managing one of the hotel salons, Mrs. Christenson."

She hoped her prospective landlady wouldn't look down her nose at someone who wasn't a corporate executive by twenty-five. Why Mrs. Christenson wanted to rent a room in this gorgeous house remained a mystery.

"Call me Olivia, dear." The woman leaned forward, expectant. "In what hotel?"

"The Fontaine." Kitty paused a moment for the woman's reaction. "I start there next week." She held her breath. If she didn't get the room, she'd have to commute from her mother's, an hour's drive. She wasn't looking forward to that.

Olivia flashed her a pleasant smile, creating little waves of wrinkles around her face. "Splendid!"

Kitty picked up a cookie and nibbled, trying to stay calm. She hadn't had breakfast and she was feeling a little light-headed.

"You probably wonder why I'm, uh, accepting a guest into my home." The woman didn't seem able to bring herself to say "renting a room." "My husband died nearly five years ago. A heart attack! And I get lonesome here in this big house by myself. I thought it might be nice to have a younger person around— the right person, of course." Her fingers locked together, eyes dimming.

"I'm sorry you lost your husband," Kitty said with sympathy. Her gaze fell on Mrs. Christenson's diamond ring. It would make even Elizabeth Taylor envious.

Mary shook her head, murmuring a condolence.

"Yes." Mrs. Christenson sighed. "A terrible blow. But we must go on."

Kitty hesitated. Maybe this wasn't such a good idea. She didn't want to intrude.

The matron gave her a wan smile. "I lead a quiet life and don't entertain with any frequency, except for my bridge club." She fixed a scrutinizing gaze on Kitty. "Do you smoke? It's important that we be compatible, don't you agree?"

"Oh, yes," Kitty replied. "I mean no, I don't smoke."

"I quite understand. Excellent. You may move in when you're ready."

Kitty barely had time to heave a sigh of relief before her mother spoke up. "About the rent . . . ."

Mrs. Christenson held up a hand. "It won't be out of line," she said. "And oh, by the way, Kitty, you wouldn't mind lending a hand now and then, would you? I could cut your, uh, fee, some. We'd help each other."

You scratch my back, I'll scratch yours, Kitty thought. *Not a bad arrangement.* She couldn't wait to tell Nate. "Fine with me."

Then she remembered she'd have to call Rick, too.

Chapter Three

After Kitty called Nate's pager to give him her new address, she left a message on Rick's answering machine. Nate called her back within the hour.

"Hey, that's great! Decent neighborhood, too."

"Decent? It's first class," she said.

"I'll help you move. Just tell me when."

"Nate, I don't know. I've been thinking . . ."

"About what?"

"Oh, never mind. I'm moving tomorrow."

"I'll be there. Eight too soon?"

Nate helped Kitty cart her suitcases and boxes upstairs in Olivia Christenson's home. He made a show of trying out the bed in her new room, and she laughed at his antics.

"Not bad." He sat up and swung his long legs to the floor.

"I like the way you understate things. This is a luxurious bedroom and you know it."

"Yeah, this house is a tad nicer than your last place. That's a given."

Kitty made a face and he grinned, shoving himself to his feet. The sunlight flooded through the windows. She sat down in a velvet peach-colored chair that flanked the fireplace, kicked off her shoes, and massaged her toes.

"An interior decorator had to have furnished this room, don't you think?"

He rubbed his unshaven jaw. "You've got me. Now that we're finished, how about lunch?" His expression was hopeful.

"I'm too much of a mess—not even a bit of lipstick."

"A drive-through, then?"

"I'll take you up on it. And thanks for everything." She leaned up and brushed a kiss across his cheek.

"What's that for?"

"For helping me bring all this stuff over here."

Nate touched his cheek and his mouth turned up in a beguiling grin.

Kitty came back from jogging on the beach before breakfast time. Perspiration stained her sweatshirt. The house lay silent. She made her way to the sunny kitchen. Her landlady's brindle-colored dog bustled in, tail wagging in an arc. She held her palm out to let the dog sniff, and he licked her hand. His muzzle was gray. When she looked up, Olivia stood framed in the doorway, smiling. She wore a pink silky bathrobe.

"Good morning, Kit, dear." She glided in, yawning,

her hair in disarray. "I see Cromwell's demanding your attention. We're the same age in dog years." She chuckled. "He's a charmer but he can be a pest, too." She leaned down and kissed the bony crown on the top of the weimaraner's sleek head.

"I hope you slept well," Kitty said. She felt self-conscious in the new surroundings.

"Yes, thank you." Olivia turned on the coffeepot switch. Cromwell trailed her as she went about her activities. "My husband always liked to name our pets after famous people. Sort of quirky, don't you think? He would never admit it was a put-down of the rich and famous."

Kitty was amused. "Clever."

When the ready signal beeped, Olivia poured coffee into bone china cups. Both had chips.

"Here. I hope it's not too strong. I buy only Jamaican Blue Mountain beans. They're the very best." Her mouth twitched. "I like your young man. Nate, isn't it?"

"Thanks for the coffee. Nate's not my boyfriend. Just a good friend." Kitty took a sip, recognizing the coffee as a bland, common supermarket variety. Did the woman live in her own dreamworld? She certainly didn't appear senile.

"That's not what his eyes tell me," Olivia said.

The first hectic week at the new salon had drawn to a close. Kitty climbed the stairs to her bedroom, head spinning with everything that had happened. She slipped out of her shoes and tossed them in a corner. The telephone rang. With Olivia's consent, she'd had a private line installed.

"Hi, Kitty. It's me, Nate. Thought I'd call and see how the new job's going. You all settled in?"

The tiredness evaporated as she flopped down on the bed pillows and cupped the receiver to her ear. "It's good to hear from you. Oh, I guess things went okay. At least they didn't fire me, although I made a few errors. Thank heavens tomorrow's Sunday."

"Want to go to the beach? The weather's too nice to sit at home."

Kitty hesitated. *Why not?* she told herself. It wasn't like it was a date or anything. "I'd love to."

"Pick you up at eleven, then. I'll stop by a deli on my way and get some sandwiches."

"I'm hungry already. Make mine tuna."

He laughed. "Still like tuna, huh? Okay, see you."

After she hung up Kitty thought about the long-forgotten days of their youth. Picnics down by the creek. Free-spirited play. School dances. She smiled at the lovely recollections.

Then, just when she was about to jump in the shower, Rick called. He said he was in a hurry but wanted to know whether she had gotten settled all right. She assured him everything was fine, but he hung up before she could tell him about the eccentric Mrs. Christenson.

On Sunday, Nate picked Kitty up and headed east. He gave her a sidelong glance. The wind from the open window caused her coppery hair to sway—and suddenly his heart did funny things. He tried to make small talk. In the past he would have rattled on about nothing in particular, but they were different people now. He didn't want to bore her. She gazed back at him, smiling. He liked that. When she replied to a question about her mom's health, he watched how her lips moved in that alluring way. Their shape could intoxicate any man, he told himself.

With Kitty back in his world, he wanted to be near her more often, but they were both so busy. He hesitated to move too fast, remembering there was a guy out there named Rick. She shot him an inquiring look as he darted in and out of traffic. Did she feel anything for him? Probably not, judging by her offhand attitude. He straightened his shoulders as they passed in front of the old Carlyle Hotel in the art deco district.

Kitty noticed two Seminole Indians, a man and a woman, dressed in traditional appliqué and patchwork clothing, and pointed them out to Nate.

"They're probably entertaining in one of the hotels," she said.

Nate wondered if the Seminole man ever experienced as much trouble as he was about to get himself into. Trying to convince Kitty she cared more for him than her boyfriend, Rick, would be a daunting challenge.

Nate stole a sidelong glance as she sat there looking out the window. He had a strong urge to say, "Kitty, darling, I can't help admiring the way the sunlight turns your hair to fire." But he didn't, thinking it would sound corny. She might even get angry. Being a policeman had taught him how to be patient—most of the time—and he'd just have to call on that discipline.

"This is a perfect day," she said. "I'm so glad you suggested it."

"The surf's up and the waves ought to be just right." He thought about the secluded beach they were going to and smiled.

"I can't remember when I went to the beach last. But now that I'm living with Mrs. Christenson, I'm planning to slip away now and then to go for an early swim. There's a beach right behind her place."

"Maybe I'll join you sometime. I noticed she had a Jacuzzi, too."

Meeting Kitty again had literally flipped his world upside-down. She was no longer the tomboy of his past, climbing trees and searching for alligator eggs with him, but a gorgeous, fascinating woman.

"Sure—sometime," she said.

They reached the shore and climbed out. The sound of the waves lapping against the sand called a peaceful welcome. In the distance seagulls gathered behind a fishing boat bobbing lazily on the water like some toy in a giant tub.

Nate heaved the cooler out of the back while Kitty picked up the beach blanket and towels. She started off across the white stretch of sand to find the perfect place, her willowy gait stirring anew the longing in him. He grinned, admiring her curves. Given time, he thought, he'd make her forget about Rick what's-his-name.

When Kitty turned and caught his look it unsettled her. He pivoted on his heels and unhooked his body-board. She spread out the blanket on the sand, hoping to get some tan, hating her fair complexion. Why couldn't she tan as golden as Nate?

He joined her, throwing down the board. "I brought a beach umbrella," he said. "No sense in frying out here."

"Great idea."

Kitty watched him hurry back to the Jeep in his cutoff jeans, his strong legs and feet churning into the sand. She realized he had probably brought the umbrella along just because of her, and she smiled to herself.

He pulled his black polo shirt over his head and tossed it in the back, then picked up the umbrella with an ease of motion.

When he came back, Kitty said, "I brought chocolate brownies. Still your favorite?" She laid the Tupperware container on top of the cooler.

"My mouth's already watering."

Kitty adjusted her wide-brimmed straw hat down over her forehead, narrowed her eyes, and watched him get things in order. She was seeing him without a shirt—as a man, and not the boy next door—for the first time. Her pulse quickened as a tingle traveled down her spine. How could she have been so blind? Embarrassed by her thoughts, she looked down at her red toenails and scrunched them into the moist warm sand, trying not to think of his well-muscled body. She looked out at the water. Meringue clouds drifted over the horizon. They looked like an artist had painted them with a light-handed stroke of the brush.

Nate set up the umbrella, ramming it into the sand, his muscles barely quivering, and tilted it so that she would be in the shade. His bare back glistened in the sun.

"Perfect. Thanks," she said.

He stood over her, suppressed excitement radiating from him. "Ready for a swim, Kitty?"

His body resembled a glorious statue, like the famous David. "Not yet. You go ahead." She wanted him to go away until she could get her emotions under control. This was not what she'd expected of herself, these roiling feelings. She had to keep their relationship platonic.

"Okay," he said, and picked up the board lying on the sand.

Kitty turned to pull out a paperback romance novel she'd tucked in her beach bag before leaving home. Assuming Nate had trotted off to the water, she decided to remove her cover-up. She rose on her knees and unbuttoned the top, pulled it over her head, and laid it aside.

"Kitty?"

"Oh!" She jumped in surprise. Nate was standing slightly back, watching her, his eyes wide with approval. Her bikini seemed too skimpy now, and the urge to put the cover-up back on hammered in her head. She sat down and burrowed into the sand beneath the blanket. He still didn't move.

"You've seen plenty of women in bikinis before," she reminded him without smiling.

He gave her a half grin. "But most of them didn't look like you."

She couldn't keep from breaking into a smile. "Go away."

"I was just going to ask when you wanted to eat."

"In an hour, say?"

"Okay with me."

Kitty turned away, ignoring him, and took out a bottle of suntan lotion. She spread it with a slight tremble of her hand over her legs. He set the board back down. When she attempted to reach around to do her back, Nate knelt on one knee. "Let me," he said.

Kitty held out the bottle. When his hand touched hers, an unexpected quiver shot through her. And she changed her mind. "I can do it, thank you."

Nate shrugged and handed it back. Then he ran off and dove into the churning ocean. Waves crashed against the sandy beach, spewing foam. Did she really want to sit on the beach alone? *Not on your life!* She jumped up and sprinted to the water. It had the desired cooling effect until Nate swam to her and grabbed her around the waist. He lifted her high in his muscular arms. She squealed. He laughed and clowned around, and she forgot she wasn't still a girl.

After the swim, they ate the sandwiches and brownies. Kitty reclined beside Nate on the blanket, sipping a soft drink. She stretched out. Nate raised himself on an elbow and brushed her nose with a gull feather. She put up her hand and playfully swatted it away.

"What were you thinking?" he asked.

She gave him a long, speculative look. "I was thinking about us."

"Oh? That sounds nice. What about us?"

"What a perfect day it is for us to be together—old friends lolling around on a quiet beach. Sort of like our yesterdays all over again. Except you've grown considerably handsomer."

"And you've grown more beautiful, if that's possible."

He leaned over to kiss her lightly. Her lips parted. She sat up, asking herself what she was doing. Yet his presence had an unsettling effect on her.

When the breeze lifted her hat almost off her head, he snatched it before it could blow away, and tried to help her put it back on. The hat landed on the bridge of her nose. She laughed. The simple act cut the tension between them.

Kitty knew she must fight her attraction to Nate. However, he didn't appear to be the sort of man easily discouraged. Casting about for something to say, she settled on, "We'd better be getting back."

"But it's early."

"I've got loads of things to do at home. Olivia needs a hand. She said she had a cleaning lady but I know now she doesn't. That's a huge house to try to keep tidy. Then there's laundry, and, oh, you know."

"I'll help you."

"Do laundry and housework?" His offer amused her. "You've got to be kidding."

He shrugged. "I volunteered, didn't I?"

"I'll take a rain check, but thanks all the same." She cleared her throat and lay back down. "Maybe we can stay just a little longer. I haven't done this in so long."

"I've been thinking about you a lot," he said. "On duty, in my Jeep . . ."

Kitty smiled. His hand covered hers and he entwined their fingers. He leaned down, a breath away from her ear, creating a growing inferno inside her heart. Restraints were slipping away faster than a hummingbird's wings could flutter.

Questions and doubts floated away with the sea breeze. Part of her wanted his arms to hold her, to shut out the world. They were two souls in the vast universe. Yet there were too many things involved. Like Rick. And Nate being a policeman.

It was then they heard the footfalls in the sand and the giggles. Two joggers, a man and a woman in their twenties, gave them a long look as they ran on along the beach.

The spell was broken. Kitty felt her face turn crimson, although they weren't even touching each other. Nate swore under his breath, his face sagging a little.

"Just when we were really relaxing, interlopers come along. Rats!"

Then a family with five children came down the path, all talking at once. *So much for the secluded beach,* she thought.

Chapter Four

Later that afternoon, when Nate dropped Kitty off, she hurried upstairs to shower. Being with him left her with a feeling of euphoria, and too many unanswered questions. They had frolicked in the surf like teenagers. If this kept up she'd have a hard time keeping the relationship where she wanted it to stay.

Why didn't Rick treat her with the same consideration as Nate did? But then, they were two different personalities.

Kitty wiggled out of the wet bikini, noted the pinkish tinge of her skin, and hoped the faint coloring would turn into a tan.

The shower restored her energy as the warm water dripped down her body. She changed into white shorts and a tank top, and went downstairs to the library looking for Olivia. When she didn't find her, Kitty called her name.

"I'm out here in the garden, dear," Olivia shouted back.

Kitty strolled through the open French doors. Olivia sat on the grass, slightly hunched over freshly planted petunias and alyssum. Perspiration ran down her forehead in narrow rivulets. She looked tired, Kitty thought with a twinge of guilt, thinking she should help more.

"You ought to have the gardener come more than twice a month," Kitty said. However, she was sorry she'd expressed her opinion as soon as the words came out of her mouth. It had become apparent Olivia couldn't afford to have him more often.

Olivia shrugged the remark away. She pushed her straw sunhat back and surveyed her handiwork. "These little flowery faces looking up at me are such a delight. They smell heavenly, don't they?"

Kitty nodded. "I wish I could capture their essence and create a fine perfume out of them. I could make a mint."

Olivia shaded her eyes. "Gardening is so therapeutic, don't you think, Kit dear?" She placed a trowel down on the grass beside the flowers and massaged her knuckles.

"You can turn anything into a positive," Kitty said.

Olivia smiled. "You don't mind my calling you Kit, do you? It suits you so much better. More business-like, too."

"Of course not. Here, let me help. My mom says gardening's good for the waistline." She rolled her eyes. Together they finished the task in the company of birds chattering and trilling from the tree branches.

* * *

On Monday morning at the salon, Kitty reflected on the things she had learned about the moneyed clients who came through the doors. They were markedly different from the steady clientele in her mother's small-town beauty shop. Kitty wasn't sure her cosmetics would ever please these sophisticated creatures. Many of them ordered every treatment the salon had to offer, in an attempt to hold back the creeping signs of age. Their tiny scars, from cosmetic surgery, were not difficult to detect by the trained eye.

The day turned warm and Kitty opened the floor-to-ceiling windows to let in the sea breeze. Potted palms and philodendrons lent an out-of-doors appearance to the place. She could hardly wait for Andrea to let her put her new cosmetics on the shelves. If her boss didn't mention it pretty soon, she'd ask for a meeting.

Financially, things had improved. Kitty now received a commission as well as salary. The rent for her room at Olivia's proved to be within reason, allaying that fear. Kitty plowed most of the money back into her fledgling business. Olivia had turned over the cellar to her to use as a lab.

Kitty looked down at her wristwatch. Rick was supposed to phone before she left and she stayed within range of the telephone. It irked her that he didn't call more often, but then Rick could be absentminded.

On the other side of town, Nate pulled up at a streetlight near a bus stop. A man and two women in their later years rested on a bench. The women wore wide-brimmed summer hats. They smiled and nodded in easy conversation. The sun glistened off the bald head of the overly tanned man. One of the women flirted with him.

Nate grinned. *You're never too old.*

The light changed and they disappeared from view. Nate realized he was in Little Havana when he passed Eighth Street. Everyone in the neighborhood called it Calle Ocho. A sign advertised PERROS CALIENTES— hot dogs. He turned down another avenue, with an image of Kitty O'Hara squarely before his eyes. He counted himself pretty rusty in the dating department. The week before he had taken her to the beach and helped her make Olivia's cellar into a cosmetics lab. Her double workload troubled him because it distanced their relationship, that and the time she spent with Rick Grant. Last night when Nate called, she gave him an excuse, saying she was just too tired to see him. It drove him crazy, especially after she mentioned Rick would be going with her to Palmella over the Christmas holidays.

"I should be the man in her life now," he growled, his words trailing in the wind from the open car window. The gut-wrenching thought of her in another man's arms caused him to press harder on the accelerator. Sure, in the beginning he had said he only wanted to be friends, but they'd moved beyond that, hadn't they?

He chided himself for dwelling on Kitty while he was on duty, thinking he needed to find his snitch, Romero. The guy left a message saying he'd be in a café on this street.

Romero promised to give him information on a shipment of illegal arms due into one of the ports soon. The man just didn't know which one yet. Nate had been working on the case for weeks.

He drove past a cigar factory and small family-run shops, clamping his teeth in frustration. Then something caught his attention in the next block over. Thick smoke snaked skyward. He floored it, taking the corner fast. He raced down the street, pulling up in front of a shabby frame house. Blackish smoke belched out of the windows and open front door. A young dark-haired woman ran toward him, her eyes wild with fear.

"Señor! Mi niño, mi niño!" She waved her hands in the direction of the house, then hurriedly moved her arms as though she were cradling a baby. Nate got the picture. There wasn't even time to call in an alarm. An old woman, dressed in black, crossed herself, then let loose a bloodcurdling scream that sent him into action.

Nate flew out of the Jeep and dashed to the house. With his eyes already burning, he knew he had to act fast. He heard a siren wail in the distance. But this firetrap wouldn't wait. Shouldering his way into the smoke-filled living room, he tripped over a guitar and swore, then dropped down on his hands and knees to where the air was still breathable. It wouldn't be for long.

He crawled along the hall, breathing shallowly, and turned into the first doorway. It was then that he heard a whimper. He rose to his feet and immediately broke into a coughing fit. His throat felt as though he was belching fire, and his eyes stung. The air was like breathing the inside of a closed barbecue grill.

By the time he found the crib, he was gasping. The hairs on his arms had turned black. He reached into the crib and grabbed a limp toddler, steeling himself not to panic.

Crouching low, the toddler silent in his arms, he

staggered out of the room. Searing flames licked one side of the living room, fast becoming an inferno by the time he was halfway across the floor. Fearing the water heater might explode at any minute, he dove out the front door in a rolling motion, protecting the child against his chest. Then tunnel vision set in. Everything went blank and he collapsed into oblivion, no longer noting the screams.

When Nate awoke in a hospital bed and lifted his head, the first thing he asked was, "Did the kid make it?"

A woman wearing white slacks and a hospital coat nodded. "I'm Dr. Hopper. And yes, the tyke made it all right. Thanks to you, Lieutenant."

He eased back down. "How long have I been here?"

"Since yesterday."

Nate glanced at his watch and realized his arms were covered in white bandages. He raised up on his elbows. "I've got to get out of here! Need to find a guy fast."

"You heroes!" She laughed. "All alike. But you're not going anywhere. Smoke inhalation. Just stay put. I'm calling the shots here, my friend."

"Want to bet on it?" He sat up, threw the sheet off, then realized he was in a short hospital gown. He covered himself as best he could, then stepped down, only to slump. The doctor caught him before he fell.

"I win the bet," the doctor said. Unsmiling, she helped him back to the side of the bed.

Kitty stopped for gas on the way home from work, then slid back into her car and switched on the radio to a local station. Her hands smelled like gasoline and she rolled down a window for fresh air. She hadn't heard from Nate in several days, which shocked her all the more when his name was mentioned over the radio airwaves. At first the unexpected news didn't register.

"Lt. Nate Mansfield of the Miami Police Department has been released from the hospital today. He will receive an outstanding meritorious citation for bravery beyond the call of duty," the announcer said. "Lt. Mansfield rushed into a burning house and saved a small child. The mayor's office is planning . . ."

My gosh! When did he go to the hospital? And why didn't he tell me?

A chill ran down her spine. Nate in danger. She remembered he'd left a message on her answering machine but she had been waiting for Rick to call and didn't want to tie up the line. What a fool she'd been.

Kitty drove to Olivia's in a state of near panic. When she arrived, she jumped out of the car, almost forgetting the keys, and hurried inside to the telephone in the library to dial Nate's number. The answer phone came on. Adrenaline raced through her. She waited for five minutes, unable to sit down, then tried again. Still no answer. She left a terse message.

"Nathan, why haven't you called? And what's this about a fire? Call—hear?"

She blamed herself, knowing he had tried, *You're the one who didn't bother to answer his call, you goose.*

Later that evening, Nate rang Kitty. Relief flooded over her.

"I can't believe you finally answered." His tone was flat.

"What happened to you? I heard something on the radio about you being involved in a rescue."

"Nothing much happened." He clammed up.

"The mayor's going to give you a citation. I think that's something, all right."

"Just standard stuff. They'll pat my head and give it to me at the department's monthly meeting."

"Oh, you never want to talk about your work! Will you come over tomorrow night for dinner?"

"Sure. I never pass up a home-cooked meal." The timbre of his voice lightened.

"Good. Come at seven. See you then." She hung up. Nate, a hero!

Olivia came into the library. "Hello, Kit, dear." She sat down in her favorite chair and switched on the television to CNN. "Why don't you join me? You look positively haggard."

Kitty scratched her head. "I'm sort of in a quandary, Olivia. I invited Nate to join us for dinner tomorrow. I didn't think you'd mind. You said it wouldn't be a problem if I had him over sometime."

"Of course not. A fine young man—quiet and emotionally strong."

She told Olivia about the news report. The older woman was visibly moved. "I'm very impressed."

"I'm so proud of him," Kitty said. "But what if he had been killed?"

"Don't borrow trouble, Kit, dear. Nate's head is firmly on his shoulders. He'll be fine."

Common sense told her she couldn't afford to get too close to him, but her heart told her something else.

"I have a problem, Olivia. I can't cook worth a darn. Nate'll be expecting a meal like my mom used to cook."

"Oh, dear! A frozen dinner won't do. You know I can't do much more than open a can of soup or scramble a batch of eggs. I wish I had my cook, Pauline, again. Wonderful woman. Oh, the fabulous dinner parties my husband and I used to throw. Dozens of people would come. Even the mayor came once." She looked dreamily off into space.

"Sunday's Nate's birthday. We could make it a small surprise party with a cake and maybe presents."

Olivia plucked herself out of her reverie. "A lovely idea. Let's put on our thinking caps. How about your asking Estella to cook?"

Kitty frowned. Olivia had finally broken down and hired a real cleaning lady to come in twice a month. "He's a meat-and-potatoes kind of guy. I don't see him eating Puerto Rican food."

"More's the pity," she said. "It's quite delicious."

Kitty agreed.

Olivia's lips turned up. "I must admit I think he's a good-looking man. Just because I'm older doesn't mean I don't notice things. You better not let him slip away, Kit."

"Now, Olivia, we're only longtime friends. Let's concentrate on the dinner. Any more ideas?"

She looked down at her folded hands briefly, then her eyes widened. "Takeout, dear. That's what you ought to do."

"Takeout? Like burgers and pizza? I'm sure that wouldn't be a treat for a bachelor."

Olivia smiled. "Of course not. I mean ordering from a restaurant and bringing it home."

"I'll do it."

* * *

On the morning of the dinner party, Kitty drove to the market early before going to work and picked up fresh salad fixings and plump pink shrimp. She reminded herself to stop on her way home from work to pick up the pot roast she'd ordered from a restaurant. Olivia had promised to go to the bakery. Knowing Nate was coming caused a sudden tremor of excitement in Kitty. She hoped everything would work out. Then she asked herself why she was so tense. After all, it was only Nate Mansfield coming to dinner.

Nate drew up in the driveway a few minutes after 7:00. He jumped out with a box of chocolates tucked under his arm and knocked at the door of the big house. Dressed in a navy blue sport coat and a long-sleeved shirt to hide the bandages, he stood back and waited impatiently. He'd even made the ultimate sacrifice of getting out the iron to press his khaki slacks.

Kitty opened the door and gazed at him. A smile spread across her face in a most enticing way. He let his eyes travel over her, from her coppery hair down to her sandals, then handed her the chocolates with a grin.

"Hey, Kitty. You look great."

She accepted both the gift and the compliment. "Come in. Thanks for this." She tilted her head, held up the box, and stepped back to let him stroll into the foyer as she gave him a closer look. "I've never seen you dressed so sharp, except on prom night, that is. Very nice. Where're your blue jeans?"

Nate grinned but didn't reply. On impulse, he pushed back a strand of her hair that had fallen over one eye. The texture was as soft as a cashmere sweater. Kitty thanked him again and brushed a feather-light kiss against his cheek. He caught the subtle scent of her perfume. It stirred his brain as delicious thoughts of her spun around crazily. They linked arms.

It was then Kitty noticed the bulk of bandages and his bound hands with only the fingers showing.

"Nate, you're hurt."

"Now, don't make a big thing over it. I just have to wear these darn things a few more days."

"Oh, you must be in pain. I . . ."

The worry on her face made him give a deep sigh. "Let's not talk about it now. Okay?"

"But . . ."

He locked eyes with hers. "Enough said. I'm fine— believe me."

Kitty let it drop and they headed down the hall, but she couldn't stop herself from adding, "I remember when you climbed up on the back of a horse in Jimmy Edward's paddock, minus saddle and bridle. You'd never been on one in your life. I stood there holding my breath, picturing you breaking your neck. The horse did some quick moves, stepped sideways, and tossed its head. Then it sort of humped up in the middle and kicked out with its back legs. You went flying and hit the ground—just lying there, not moving a muscle. Scared me half out of my mind. I thought, 'He's dead. Oh, my gosh, what'll do now?' "

"You still remember that?"

She nodded. "Finally, you sat up, dusted yourself off, and tried to climb back on. You would have, too, if I hadn't started crying. Now you saved a child. Am I surprised? No. You always were a Sir Galahad type of guy."

Nate found himself grinning. "What an overactive

imagination you have. I don't recall it being that way at all."

They entered the library. He took Olivia's hand and gave it a small squeeze. "Nice to see you again, Mrs. Christenson. Thanks for having me over."

"We're happy you could come. Call me Olivia. Let's not stand on formality." She indicated that he should sit in her late husband's leather wingback chair, and he complied.

"Nice," he said, settling in it.

Kitty had mixed pineapple and guava drinks. She glanced at him as she poured from the pitcher on the table. Olivia was talking to him. He caught Kitty observing him and winked.

Dinner passed without a glitch. The roast she had ordered from the restaurant was perfect. Afterward, they sat around the table drinking coffee. With some prompting, Nate told them how he had come upon the burning house and the frantic women. He made it sound like it was all in a day's work.

Olivia said, "How brave."

He looked uncomfortable. "It wasn't anything, really."

"But you saved a child's life. I certainly don't call that nothing," Olivia persisted.

Nate could see that Olivia had been an attractive woman in her day and she still had plenty of charm. He liked the twinkle in her eye and her rich laugh.

Olivia switched the conversation to Kitty's new job. "I'm glad things are going smoother at the salon, Kit. But you work too hard." She turned her attention back to Nate "This young woman comes home and starts all over again down in her cellar lab."

Kitty waved it off. "Let's hear more about your work, Nate."

His smile faded. "You'd find it tiresome."

Kitty noticed his thick eyelashes were singed, and a stab of worry tore through her. She set her coffee cup on the table.

"Law enforcement sounds so exciting," Olivia said. "You must tell us more."

"Police work is more than catching criminals, although most people don't think so," he said. "There's a lot of checking on statements and waiting around."

Olivia looked grave. "Be honest. Weren't you frightened when you entered that burning house? I would have been terrified."

His face took on a serious cast. "Yeah. I was—sure. I admit my heart did some drumrolls and I had to remind myself to keep calm. Now—enough. Let's talk about something else." He turned to Kitty. "How's your business coming along? Have you talked your boss into letting you sell your cosmetics in her salon?"

His intense gaze melted Kitty like a marshmallow, and she sank back deeper into the chair. "Not yet. But I'm working on her. They're selling pretty well in two other shops. But government regulations prevent me from doing much else until I can expand."

"My life seems so tame compared to you two," Olivia said. "However, last week a friend of mine's husband came out of a tobacco shop. A young man jostled him. It was only after Dan reached home that he missed his wallet. Tell me, how does such a thing happen so fast?"

Nate scratched his ear. "Pickpockets walk by, brush against a person, barely making contact. The guy may not even have felt it, but he's now relieved of his wallet. The pickpocket passes it to another dude a few feet away who hides it in a newspaper. Magic! He's no longer carrying the wallet—just in case he gets fingered by the victim. Happens all the time."

"Oh, my." Olivia's brows furrowed and she made little clucking sounds. "One has to be so careful these days."

Kitty rose. "We've cross-examined Nate long enough. It's time for his birthday cake."

"Birthday cake! How in the world . . . ? I'm amazed you remembered." He shot her a broad grin.

Kitty laughed and hurried to the kitchen. She brought back a cake with lemon icing and a circle of blazing candles.

"Make a wish." She placed it in front of him.

"My favorite. What a memory." Nate looked slightly embarrassed as he blew out the candles, reminding Kitty for a brief moment of when he was a boy.

"Some things people don't forget." She cut thick slices, promising herself she'd diet tomorrow.

He took a mouthful. "Real good," he said and bit into another.

When they finished, she brought out presents, handing him the two boxes. These presents first."

He grinned. "This is too much." Without taking his eyes off of her, he unwrapped the one with the bright plaid ribbon. When he opened it, he threw his head back and laughed, his voice a rich deep timbre.

"No! I can't believe it," he bellowed heartily.

He took out a small Red Baron aviator cap and toy goggles. Kitty couldn't stop laughing.

"All I need now is Snoopy," he said.

"And the Red Baron's crimson Fokker triplane.

Sorry, but I couldn't find one," Kitty said. "I remember how you loved watching that old movie about the Red Baron—the one with Robert Redford. You said you were going to be a pilot, just like him, even though the Red Baron was the enemy."

He nodded, smiling at the recollection. "Great gift, Kitty. Just what I needed."

She handed him the other one. "Try this on."

He met her eyes, and she observed an unguarded emotion there before his hooded eyes switched back to the gift. "You're spoiling me," he said. He lifted out underwater goggles and slipped them on. "Perfect. I'll use them next time I go snorkeling."

"And this is from me," Olivia said in her breezy way. She handed him another brightly wrapped gift.

Nate opened it and thanked her for the box of initialed handkerchiefs.

"Very fancy. I'll be sure to take one along when I go to someplace special." His grin widened. "You two really put one over on me. I don't quite know what to say. Dinner. Presents. Thank you both." He bent over the table and brushed a kiss across Kitty's cheek, then Olivia's.

They adjourned to the library, and Olivia's eyes fluttered sleepily after a little while. She excused herself and retired.

After she was gone, Nate stretched and got to his feet. "Want to take a walk on the beach?"

"Sounds like a perfect idea."

He pulled Kitty out of the chair and gave her a light hug. "It's been a really nice evening."

"Maybe we can walk off a few of the calories in that cake." She chuckled.

They exited through the French doors and out beyond the garden to the beach. Kitty slipped off her sandals and let them dangle from her fingers, feeling rejuvenated and free in the soft ocean breeze.

Following her instincts, she danced joyfully to the edge of the water. "I feel like a moon goddess." She let her figure sway rhythmically to the music playing in her head.

Nate stood back, watching her, his hands thrust in his pockets. "You're more beautiful than ever, Kitty," he said, his voice just above a whisper.

She started to reply, but her voice caught in her throat, as strong feelings threatened to break loose.

The night was luminously brightened by a moon so filled with gold Kitty thought it would burst open and shower down upon them. She came back to where he stood and stared up at his parted lips. A look of longing was in his eyes. When he reached out, she realized a man's strength held her, not the boy of the past.

His arms tightened and he kissed the curve of her neck. His warm lips descended to hers, and he gave her a mind-altering kiss that left her limp.

She didn't quite understand this mad stirring of longing but she wanted him to keep on kissing her, forcing away the niggling thought of Rick that threatened to surface.

Nate barely let her catch her breath, then captured her willing lips again. He tenderly covered her cheeks and eyelids and nose with delightful kisses and nibbles, ending with a playful tug on her earlobe.

"Oh, Nate," she whispered.

He hugged her so close she could feel the rapid beats of his heart. Then he buried his face in her hair. "Darling, I adore you so much," he said, his voice husky.

Rapturous emotion swept over Kitty like a giant ocean wave. This man, little by little, was stealing her heart. The love in her threatened to overwhelm reason.

All at once she felt she would faint if he didn't stop his kisses, and she turned her face away. Wrestling with unrequited feelings, she murmured, "No, Nate!"

He pushed her back gently, but didn't release her. His astonished eyes examined the details of her face in the moonlight. "What? No?"

"I . . . I love Rick. It's not fair to him." She managed to get out the words, even though she wasn't convinced it had ever been true.

At first Nate didn't reply. Then his features grew rigid with suppressed fury, his tone filled with authority. "Excuse me! You're telling me you love another guy when you respond to me like this? Be straight with me, Kitty—and yourself. What you said is crazy and you know it."

Kitty cringed when she stammered, "I—I admit I'm attracted to you—but that's not enough."

Nate looked as though she had slapped him, and his eyes flashed.

"Kitty O'Hara, you're not telling the truth!"

She fought to hold back the flood of tears welling behind her eyes. "Okay. I do care about you. I'll concede that. But there's Rick. And you're a cop. You're confusing me!"

Nate turned away, as though to collect himself. Kitty glanced up at his marvelously sculpted profile and for an instant wanted him to take her back in his arms. His kisses had awakened her longing for him like she never would have believed. She wanted back the intoxicating sensations she'd experienced, even while she fought them. She'd never felt that way about

Rick. But nevertheless they had a commitment. She reminded herself that Rick had helped finance the start of her business. He came from a wealthy family, even though she hadn't become interested in him because of that.

A cloud passed over the moon and darkness enveloped them. Nate brusquely took her in his arms. This man who held on to her with such resolve was far more complex than she had ever imagined. Now he was being aggressively male, and it surprised her that she wasn't infuriated. The easygoing Nate of another decade was now a man with commanding energy and determination. His intense eyes locked her in his own space as though she were a prisoner. She couldn't escape the pulsating emotion—old as time—that speeded up her heartbeat.

"Darling, we belong together. Don't you understand that?" His deep, caressing voice made it hard for her not to surrender as he went on murmuring endearments into her ear.

"You're driving me out of my mind," he murmured. "Don't you know it's always been you? I'm tired of playing this silly 'old friend' role you seem to want to box me into."

His depth of feeling moved something deep inside her. He covered her lips with a kiss that thrilled her down to her toes. But she pulled away, fearing she would drown in emotion if he continued.

Her final rejection precipitated a roaring argument.

"Darn it, Kitty! You're playing games with me!"

"I am not!"

"Yes, you are! Didn't you kiss me back? If I mean nothing more than a 'physical' body to you, why did you even let me kiss you in the first place?"

"I . . . I don't know. Maybe I was just lonely."

"Lonely? If that's a cockamamie excuse."

She cut in brutally. "I told you about Rick Grant."

"You belong to me. Admit it!" He enveloped her in his arms.

"No, I don't! Besides, you went off to college and forgot all about me. I'll bet you dated every girl that caught your eye."

He took a sizable breath, then exhaled. "You were only sixteen, darling. Besides, you never answered my letters."

"Nate Mansfield, you knew I didn't want you to become a law enforcement officer but you did it anyway!"

"It was something I had to do. And as it turns out, I'm pretty good at my job."

The anger seemed to drain from him, replaced by searing hurt. "You're impossible."

He released her, turned on his heel, and walked stiffly away, his head down, leaving her alone on the beach. She dabbed at the blinding tears and sank down on the sand to have a good cry. One thing she was sure of, she'd never marry a cop and spend her life worrying whether he'd come home at night or end up in the morgue. She wouldn't make the same mistake her mother had made.

Chapter Five

That night, just when Kitty was on the verge of falling asleep, Nate's face drifted back into her consciousness, tormenting her with questions she didn't want to answer. It wasn't as though he was the first good-looking guy with charisma and ambition to stride into her life. But he was different. She'd met enough men with king-sized egos, but no heart, to know the difference. Now he'd touched her at a very profound level, whether she chose to admit it or not.

Kitty regretted that the birthday party had ended in a squabble, and she wondered if he would ever call her again. Why did he want what she couldn't give him? It suddenly occurred to her that perhaps she was using Rick as the excuse to keep Nate at arm's length.

On Wednesday morning, Nate called Kitty. She sounded standoffish.

"I'm sorry I lost my temper the other night. Just call me a jerk," he said.

"I guess there was just too much moonlight." Her voice softened. "It can do funny things to people."

Her determination to discount the feelings they'd shared angered him all the more and he wanted to lash out, but he kept his cool. "Yeah. How about dinner to show there's no hard feelings?"

She hesitated, then agreed to meet him after work.

When Nate saw Kitty coming toward him in the lobby of the hotel, something twisted around his heart. He rose to his feet. Without knowing quite how to approach her, he waited for her to make the first move.

"Hi. How are things going?" Her voice sounded like crystal wind chimes. "Arms all healed?"

"Yeah, the bandages came off today." He cleared his throat.

"That's good."

A hostess led them to a table in the lounge. He waited for Kitty to take a seat. Then a waitress appeared at his elbow, waiting to take their orders.

"I'll have Perrier," Kitty told her.

Nate ordered coffee. The waitress hurried away and returned before they'd said more than a handful of words. Kitty took a sip. The way her upper lip faintly touched the rim of the glass made it hard for him to pull his gaze away. She'd never know how mesmerizing that simple movement could be.

"Have a good day?" He figured that was an innocuous-enough question.

"It went fast."

When she didn't say more, he groaned inwardly.

She wasn't going to make it easy for him. "Where would you like to go for dinner?"

Any place you choose."

Why couldn't she say 'lets eat Chinese food tonight, or Cuban or Mexican or Hungarian,' for heaven sake.

Her eyes studied him. "How about going some place for seafood?"

"I know a restaurant close by that's got great swordfish."

They finished their drinks. She told him Olivia had dropped her off that morning. Sensing her standoffishness, he didn't help her into the Jeep.

The restaurant was across Biscayne Bay, a weathered place with low lighting inside. Nate and Kitty perused the menu.

"You look terrific," he said after they had ordered.

"Thanks." Her smile wasn't relaxed enough to suit him. He was worried she was still harboring some ill feelings about the other night.

"How's your cosmetics business coming along?"

Kitty perked up. "I'm beginning to make a small profit."

She looked beautiful. Her full lips tantalized him when they curved into a smile. He watched her interest grow as she explained her new marketing ideas. She looked like a million dollars as she sparkled with excitement.

"Want to dance?" he said.

"All right."

She rose gracefully.

The easy flow of talk common to them continued to be stilted. To his dismay she acted as though the other night never happened, that she hadn't kissed him with passion.

On the small dance floor he took her in his arms, but he didn't hold her tightly. He wished fervently that he could tap into her brain—to know what she was thinking.

"I received a letter from Laurie Kingston," she said. "Remember her? She's coming home for Christmas."

"No kidding? Haven't seen Laurie since high school." With the overhead lighting aglow, her hair shone like spun gold, and he fought back an urge to run his fingers through it.

"She plans to spend a couple of days with me before going to see her folks in Palmella."

"Maybe we can all get together before then . . . have a reunion. Hey, there's a country western tavern over in Fort Lauderdale. Think she'd like that?"

"Uh-huh. I know she would," Kitty said. "Laurie always loves a party."

A recording of an old Cole Porter song played over the sound system. *"Night and Day, you are the one . . . "* He sang the words softly in her ear, encircling her small waist. The words struck him as being so true. " *. . . only you beneath the stars and under the sun . . . "*

She turned her head slightly and her lips were inches from his. "It feels so good to be dancing with you again," he said while brushing a kiss against her cheek. "Are you still mad at me?"

She didn't reply right off, then said, "No. You were probably right. I'll try not to play games anymore."

The warm curve of her spine under his palm made him crazy. "I shouldn't have said that. It was stupid. Forgive me." Confessing his need had almost killed their friendship. When would he learn to go slow with this woman?

"Nothing to forgive. Let's forget it." The strain on her face dissolved into a smile.

Nate, unable to help himself, drew her closer and she didn't resist. He bent his head, and on impulse lightly stroked her earlobe with his lips. Kitty was the woman for him. It only remained to convince her of the fact.

She stepped back. "Nate, let's not start this again."

"Yeah. Sorry."

The music changed to a fast tempo. She seemed to welcome it, throwing her head back while dancing to the rhythm.

Kitty liked dancing with Nate. With the moves of an athlete, he wasn't stiff like some men. She relished the faster pace. It helped to clear her mind of the impact of his teasing lips. Dancing so close during the last song had aroused a trifle too much tension between them. *Face it,* she told herself. *Keeping him at arm's length is going to prove to be a trial.*

When they returned to the table, Kitty held her glass to the candle in the center, observing the fragmented shards of light. It had a hypnotizing effect. She tried desperately to keep their conversation light while they ate the delicious swordfish.

What was she going to do about Nate—or Rick, for that matter? She knew she could never marry Rick now. Serious questions demanded serious thought, and she told herself she'd make them in the New Year. She ought to break it off with both of them: Rick, because she didn't really love him, and Nate, because she'd vowed never to marry a cop and spend her life worrying.

Kitty looked up at him while he ate. "How did you get that scar near your temple?" She surpressed an urge to run a finger over it.

"It's a long story." He smiled, apparently disinclined to go on.

His reluctance heightened her interest. "Tell me."

"Oh, a couple of years back I arrested a gang member. This happened while I was relieving the guy of his switchblade." Nate cracked a rye grin, finding humor in the incident. "He came close to relieving me of my ear." But his grin faded. "It galls me that the perp was back out on the street in no time."

Kitty grimaced. "When a criminal gets off and you're the arresting officer, aren't you afraid he'll come after you?" The very idea made her blood turn cold and she pushed her plate away.

He didn't answer at first, just sat looking at her. "I'm scaring you. Come on, let's dance again. But no, I don't worry about that."

Nate entwined his fingers in hers leading her back to the dance floor. The music heightened her emotional connection to him, and she realized spending so much time with him was not a good idea.

"They're playing your elevator music, Kitty." His smile came on slowly.

Kitty chuckled. "You remembered."

"I remember a lot of things."

He placed his cheek against hers. She felt herself respond to the light, prickly texture of his day-old whiskers as they slow-danced. Her heart fluttered.

When they came back to the table, Kitty said she ought to be going. Nate signaled the waitress.

Outside in the moonlight, he linked arms with hers as they headed for his Jeep.

"Nate, I know I'm bossy," Kitty said, reflecting on her own shortcomings, "selfish and downright irritating sometimes, but—"

"You know what I see?" he interrupted. "I see a warm, tender, loving gal." His eyes sparkled.

Kitty experienced a roller coaster of conflicting emotions. She looked down at the crack in the driveway, and all of a sudden she felt like crying. "I do value our longtime friendship."

He didn't smile. "Friendship is only a part of what I want from you, Kitty."

"Friendship is all it can ever be, Nate. You know that."

Nate drove her home. He stopped near the gate and leaned across her to open the door.

"Good night," he said, staying seated.

"Good night—and thanks. I had a nice time." She jumped out and blew him an air kiss.

His face broke into a grin. He slid off the seat and walked her to the door. But he didn't try to kiss her good night. He tipped his fingers to his forehead in a mock salute and turned away without looking back. She chuckled, thinking it was the sort of silly thing he did when they were kids. He could always amuse her. She stood watching until his Jeep was out of sight.

"Darn you, Nate! What am I going to do with you?"

Christmas was almost here and gaining on her. Kitty planned to spend several days with Rick, and she wouldn't see Nate at all. She reminded herself she was happy and couldn't wait to see Rick. Yet a feeling of irritation inveigled its way into her thoughts. Rick's neglect left too many unanswered questions. Sure, he worked long hours, but he wasn't the only one. Did he still love her? She no longer knew in her heart. However, when Nate was around, she had no doubt about the way he felt. He called her nearly every night. Rick called once a week.

Kitty met Rick for lunch at an open-air restaurant at the Lincoln Road Mall, a strip of art galleries, eateries, and art deco–collectible shops, where "rollercops" patrolled on in-line skates.

They sat along the walk in an inside enclosure and ordered salads. The day was particularly warm even for Florida. Kitty looked out at the well-toned women and men dressed in summer wear and wished she had the time to be a free spirit. The vacationers rolled in and out among the tourists on their skates.

"You look a little tired, Kitty." His eyes shone with concern.

"Uh-oh, you noticed, Doc." She grinned. "I envy these people spending a leisure afternoon here. If I didn't have this driving need to make a success of my business, I could join them every day. Maybe I'm a little touched in the head."

"You know I've got plenty of income for the both of us."

"It's something I have to do on my own."

Rick ran a finger over the back of her hand. "How have you been? I'm afraid I've neglected you terribly these past few months."

"There's something I've been meaning to talk to you about," she said in earnest.

He frowned, and took off his glasses, wiping them with the table napkin.

"Can't it wait until we're together during the holidays?" he said. "I see so little of you. Let's not think of anything too serious."

She dropped her plan to tell him about Nate, and glanced at her watch instead. "I've got to be getting back to the salon."

His eyes mellowed. "I'll call you soon."

"Good. I'll be looking forward to it."

They seemed to have so little to say to each other, she thought when they parted company.

Andrea Webster, who owned the salon where Kitty worked, called her into the inner office. Tension started between Kitty's eyes and shot up to the top of her head. Everything had been going so well. Did this mean she was being fired? Oh, no! How would she pay for the new pearlized jars Olivia had insisted she order for the cosmetics? And how would she repay Rick? Now that she was seeing Nate, she felt the need to get out from under that obligation as soon as possible.

"Kit, sit down. Some of my clients have been telling me you're actually manufacturing your own cosmetics. Is that true?" Andrea didn't smile.

"Well, yes, I am." Kitty reminded Andrea politely that she had already told her when she first came to work.

"You're so young. It's hard to believe you have a line of cosmetics."

"I grew up in the business," Kitty said with pride. "My mother and I developed our own formulas for her beauty shop. And I have a degree in chemistry."

"I'm astounded! Several clients say yours are better than those we buy from our distributor." The woman sat behind her carved Rococo desk, her shrewd eyes calculating. "Now tell me, how did these people find out about them? You advertise?"

Here it comes, Kitty thought. "Some of the ladies play bridge with my, er, aunt and belong to the same garden club and book group. They order them through her."

"I guess word gets around—the grapevine."

Kitty didn't mention anything about the other two salons that sold them.

"Small world. Well, could you let me have a sample or two? We might try them out. Why not! If they are as good as everyone says, we'll both benefit from our arrangement." She smiled, her finely plucked eyebrows arching.

Kitty was beside herself with excitement, but kept outwardly calm.

"Thank you. I would appreciate the opportunity to demonstrate my line. I'll bring samples in on Monday. And thanks again!" She stood up and practically floated out of Andrea's office.

Kitty called Nate that night to tell him. "I'm a happy camper. My chance at the big time is finally on the horizon. I can just see my products in some department stores."

"It's Kismet. I'll bet you danced around like someone possessed. I'd buy all your stuff in a heartbeat if I were a woman."

She chuckled.

"When am I going to see you again?"

"I'm free tonight.'

"Darn! I pulled duty."

"Call me when you're free. We'll get together—for old times' sake."

"It'll probably be four in the morning. Are you sure you want to talk to me then, Kitty?"

"On second thought, don't call me. Remember my friend Laurie from high school? She's flying in from California tomorrow for a visit."

"Whatever you say, darling."

"Nate, you shouldn't call me darling."

"Okay, darling. Good night." He broke the connection.

Laurie Kingston flew into Miami. When Kitty saw her hurrying from the ramp at the airport, she waved furiously to get her attention. They reached out to each other, hugging like sisters.

"I can't believe you're finally here," Kitty cried, jubilant. "You've let your hair grow long. That blond shade is just right. You look positively terrific! I'm so happy to see you."

"Me, too. The flight took forever. We were backed up out there on the tarmac. Sorry you had to wait so long."

"No problem. You're here now. Let's get your bags."

Laurie's well-cut white jumpsuit revealed a shapely figure. The little saddlebags on her thighs that had once plagued her were gone. When she caught Kitty staring, she said, "Liposuction! Does wonders! Try it."

Kitty started to stammer a reply, but Laurie cut her off. "We've got loads to talk about."

"How you've changed!" Kitty said. "Sophisticated, dare I say chic, right down to your designer platform sandals."

Laurie laughed. "There's a super little discount shop right off Rodeo Drive in Beverly Hills, and . . ." Soon the old familiar Laurie emerged as she related her shopping forays.

In a little while Kitty turned into Olivia's driveway. Laurie exclaimed, "Some digs! Looks like a movie set for *Sunset Boulevard*. You get along fine with the old gal, you say?"

"Olivia's really nice," Kitty replied, "although I think she's trying to make me over. And she insists on telling people I'm her niece."

Laurie grinned. "She's the grandmotherly type?"

"Not on your life."

Kitty parked the car in the garage. They got out and crossed under the rose arbor at the side of the house.

Laurie glanced around and lowered her voice when they stepped inside the foyer. "So Mrs. Christenson's rich, then?" And in the same breath, asked, "How come she took in a boarder?"

"Past tense about her being rich, I'm afraid. But she'll never admit it."

Kitty led her friend into the library, where Olivia reclined in her favorite chair. The late afternoon sun streamed through the French windows, warming her shoulders. Dozing, her eyelashes fluttered, then snapped open when she heard Kitty's voice.

"Olivia, this is Laurie Kingston. We went to school together."

Olivia's face creased into a pleasant smile and they shook hands. "I'm so happy to meet you at last, Laurie. We're thrilled to have you. Kit speaks so highly of you. I understand you're a movie star."

Laurie burst into laughter. "Oh, I wish that were true. No. Somehow I manage to keep getting the character roles. But that's okay. Someday, maybe."

"Remember what Scarlett said?" Kitty grinned. " 'Tomorrow is another day.' "

Laurie pinched her playfully on the arm. "I've heard that a thousand times."

"We have a pitcher of tropical fruit juice if you're thirsty," Olivia said kindly.

"I just had something on the plane. Thanks all the same."

Kitty couldn't wait to hear what secrets her friend had to share. A new love, perhaps? For Laurie that wouldn't be too surprising. She changed men like she changed her brand of perfume.

Olivia gave them a regal smile. "You two go along now."

Later, after dinner, Kitty took Laurie back to her bedroom. They sat beside the unlit fireplace, legs tucked up under them, filling in each other on their present lives.

"I'm so proud of you, Kitty—I mean Kit." Laurie yawned. "To tell you the truth I've dropped the little Laurie thing myself. I'm now Laura Kingston, except to you and the folks, of course."

"Olivia thinks Kit makes me sound more 'woman of the world,' " she said, amused. "Let's hear about you and Hollywood."

"I saw Mel Gibson in the commissary. You wouldn't believe how handsome he is in real life. I dropped my fork, on purpose, and he leaned over and picked it up. I nearly died right then and there."

"You look awfully happy. Are you still dating that same guy? I think you called him Michael in your letter?"

"No! He turned out to be a real turkey! You can't

trust stuntmen. They're so . . . quick. They love their fiery cars and pyrotechnics."

"Did I tell you I've seen Nate Mansfield several times since I moved here?" She tried to keep her voice casual.

"Nate from back home?"

"He's a policeman now."

"Would you believe it? But then, I recall his father was the sheriff when we were kids."

Kitty cleared her throat. "Nate's an undercover cop, and he's invited us to go to a dance tomorrow night, if you want to go, that is. A little reunion, he called it."

"Super! It'll be fun seeing him again. Is he bald, or chubby?"

Kitty grinned. "Neither. He's handsome in a very masculine way."

"Ah. Are you interested in him?"

"Of course not—not that way. You know I'm practically engaged."

She realized she'd said it too quickly when Laurie raised her brows.

Chapter Six

Kitty and Laurie drove to Fort Lauderdale to meet Nate at Joe's Corral, a western-style café and dance hall. The place's popularity never seemed to diminish. It was just as crowded and raucous tonight as the other time Kitty had been there. Sawdust and peanut shells littered the floor, and the room gave off a sweet, pungent smell of hickory chips.

Kitty nervously fingered the Indian beads that hung from the sleeve of her white denim jacket. She ran a hand down the front of her long black leather skirt, hoping she looked all right. It was so tight around the waist that caution told her not to eat too much. She hoped she hadn't overdone the western dress. A three-piece band was playing a do-si-do number as she looked around for Nate.

Her breath quickened when she saw him threading between crowded tables toward them. He wore a plaid western shirt and jeans that tapered in the waist, em-

phasizing his broad shoulders. His black cowboy hat
eased down over his forehead. He could have stepped
right out of a movie western.

Kitty waved. "Over here, Nate."

A spark flashed between them as he took long, pur-
poseful strides and came up to them. His face broke
into a wide grin, his eyes traveling over her, and he
let out a low whistle.

"Wow! It's you, Kitty! Queen of the cowgirls."

"Hi." She drew on every ounce of self-control, not
wanting him to see how glad she was to see him. "I
like your hat, cowboy."

He stood with his booted feet planted wide apart,
thumbs stuck in his back pockets, and appraised her.

"Gorgeous—you look downright gorgeous. All we
need is a surrey with the fringe on the top and we
could ride into the sunset while you sing *Oklahoma*."

Kitty laughed. "Thanks, but I sing off-key. You'd
have to do the vocal stuff." She turned. "You remember Laurie Kingston."

His gaze fell on his old high school acquaintance.
"Of course. Laurie!" They exchanged friendly hugs.
"Good to see you. Kitty said you were coming. This
is like our own homecoming. Just great! Remember
Eric Jamison? Linebacker on the football team? He's
here, too. Come on back. I have a booth there in the
corner." He gestured over his shoulder.

Laurie posed for a moment, her mouth slightly
open. "I remember you, Nate. You were always telling
jokes I didn't understand." She giggled. "I can't believe you've turned into such a handsome hunk!"

Nate winked. "Just a country boy," he said. "Don't
let this weekend cowboy getup fool you. I haven't got
a horse waiting for me at the hitching rail out front,

and the last time I was on one I got bucked off." He winked at Kitty.

Laurie gave another delighted giggle, throwing Nate a coy grin. They followed him back to the booth. Kitty chewed her lower lip. Did she see a gleam of chemistry there between them? Nate reintroduced Eric Jamison and they exchanged more hugs. Kitty barely recognized him. He'd put on weight. Laurie hustled in close next to Nate, an action not lost on Kitty.

Eric's broad, good-natured face traveled from Kitty to Laurie. "Gee! Who would have thought you gals would turn out to be so pretty. But then, I remember those football games with you two cheerleaders jumping up and down, hollering your lungs out. You made it difficult for us football players to tend to the game."

They laughed. A waitress, dressed in a short skirt, western shirt, and cowboy hat, came to take their orders.

"All we've got is chili and sandwiches, hon," she said when Laurie asked for a green salad.

"Chili all around?" Nate asked. The others nodded. "And bring us plenty of peanuts."

The waitress didn't bother to write anything down but acknowledged the orders and turned away.

Nate broke into a smile. "Did you hear the one about the waitress who asked, 'Honey, what'll it be? We got about everything you'd want on the menu.' And the guy replied, 'Yeah. I see marinara sauce, mustard, and gravy stains.' "

They all groaned, and Eric swatted him on the arm. "Not that one again."

Kitty made a face. "That joke's so old it ought to be preserved in formaldehyde."

Laurie batted her long, mascara-thick lashes. "Nate,

hon, it's so wonderful to see you again—and you, too, Eric." Her eyes didn't leave Nate. "Kitty says you're a cop."

"Eric's also an officer," he said. He acted like he was going to slug Eric but grinned instead.

Eric leaned forward, took off his straw hat, and popped a breath mint in his mouth. His hair follicles were fighting a losing battle in front, making his fore-head seem extra high.

"Yeah, I'm just a beat cop. Nate, here, gets involved with all the exciting stuff. Tell 'em about last Tuesday night." When Nate looked blank, Eric said, "You know. The shoot-out at—"

Nate raised a hand. "They wouldn't be interested." He glared across the table at Eric, who got the message and squirmed in the seat.

Kitty flinched. The ominous sound of Eric's reve-lation made her insides coil, as an inner voice cried, *He was in danger!*

Laurie straightened and adjusted the neckline of her white peasant blouse. "Come on now. Tell. I'm dying to hear."

She rolled her eyes and dropped her lower lip. Her not-so-subtle play for Nate rankled Kitty. But hadn't Kitty practically given her permission? She could have been honest and said she cared for him. But how would she explain Rick, and why she hadn't broken up with him? Laurie would accuse her of intentionally keeping them dangling. Then it occurred to her—she was!

Nate cleared his throat. "I'm afraid I can't talk about my work, Laurie," he said, his voice flat. "I never dis-cuss business after hours."

"Party-pooper," she said, a tiny pout forming

around her generous mouth. "But I can just see you as a hero type out chasing bad guys."

The waitress came back with a tray. Nate poured drinks.

Kitty could see that Laurie wasn't ready to give up when her friend asked him, "Why did you choose police work? You'll tell us *that,* won't you?"

Nate put on a grave face, but his eyes were merry. "Maybe I saw too many old John Wayne movies on television when I was a kid."

Laurie looked deflated. The waitress came back with bowls of chili.

"Enough cop-talk. Let's eat," he said, grabbing a handful of crackers, then passing them around.

They turned their attention to the steaming bowls. The chili was so hot it brought tears to Kitty's eyes. She sputtered, taking a quick swallow of cold mineral water. They all chuckled, fanning their tongues and acting as though they were choking to death.

Nate said, "Do you know what stuff a hero's made out of?"

Kitty bit. "No." This was a side of him she hadn't seen in years and it delighted her.

"Salami!"

They threw him exaggerated, bored expressions and ughs.

"Okay," he said. "No more jokes."

"Only if you can come up with some new ones," Kitty said.

When they finished, Kitty and Laurie adjourned to the ladies' room to repair their lipstick. A painted cowgirl brightened the door, a FILLY sign above it. A STUD sign was on the door across the hallway.

Kitty chuckled. "I'm glad I know a little horse lingo or we might have ended up in the men's room."

"I can't believe how appealing Nate turned out to be," Laurie said. She admired her reflection in the mirror above the sink as she raised a hand to pull a loose hair away. "He's amazing. Maybe I'll marry him."

Kitty didn't think her remark was funny, but she forced a smile. Laurie might be talented and beautiful, but fidelity was not her strong point. She swept through men like Sherman through Georgia. Kitty snapped open a tube of lipstick and it went flying across the room. Without replying to her friend's comments, she retrieved it.

"You're so quiet tonight," Laurie said. "Are you sure you aren't interested in Nate?"

Kitty tried to laugh it off. "We're just good friends."

"I could develop a downright deep affection for that hunk."

Kitty hated to hear men referred to as hunks. It made them sound like slabs of meat. It was just as demeaning as some of the terms men called women, but she let her irritation go. She hadn't seen Laurie in three years and didn't want to get into an argument. After all, they were here to have a good time, weren't they?

Laurie blotted her lips, then examined the marks on the tissue with satisfaction before discarding it in a basket.

"Honestly, I didn't give the guy a second look in high school," she said.

"Yes, you did," Kitty blurted before she realized what she was saying.

One of Laurie's eyebrows lifted. "When?"

"You asked him to go to the Sadie Hawkins Day

dance, but Mabel Carpenter asked him first. You were fit to be tied."

"Oh yeah, I forgot. Hmm. He looks positively too gorgeous to be walking around loose. Maybe he has some strange habit, like sleeping with his Magnum under the pillow."

Kitty chuckled. "Really, Laurie, where do you get these notions?"

"I work in Hollywood, kiddo!"

Kitty dropped her lipstick into her purse. "We better be getting back. They might send out a squad car if we're gone too long."

Laurie shook her head and her hair swayed. "That's a good one. Well, here I come, Officer Mansfield! Hold on to your Stetson!"

Kitty swung the door open. "He's a lieutenant."

When Laurie followed her out, she suddenly realized what was eating her—jealousy!

Kitty reminded herself to lighten up. They joined the men. A bead of perspiration cascaded down in front of her ear and she wiped it away. All of a sudden she felt plain and unattractive. Laurie knew how to take advantage of her looks. Thinking back, had it ever been different?

Nate looked up, his gaze resting on Kitty. "Did I tell you girls how great it is to see you?"

Kitty met his penetrating eyes, and somehow she knew he meant her. His words lifted her spirits. "Yes, you did," she replied.

Laurie eyed Kitty questioningly, then swept her gaze to Nate. "I'm delighted to see you and Eric, too."

The band played "Achy Breaky Heart." Eric had moved in beside Nate. Laurie sat down across from

the men and wriggled forward. "Let's dance, cowboy—
you and me."

Nate tipped his hat good-naturedly and led Laurie
to the dance floor. Kitty watched from the table as
Laurie inched her painted fingernails up his shirt front
before he drew her into his arms. Oh, how pushy Laurie could be, Kitty fumed. She lost them amidst the
boot-shod crowd.

The western music ended, but Nate and Laurie
didn't come back. Kitty looked around, letting her
eyes sift through the couples. Doubts about Nate kept
vexing her. For all she knew he and Laurie were
smooching in some dark corner. After all, neither she
nor Nate had a commitment. The thought made her
grind her teeth. The evening was passing painfully.
Renewing old friendships should be a joyful occasion.
Kitty felt like she was suffocating. It was warm in the
big room with its flashing neon signs and pictures of
horses and Brahma bulls. Her throat tightened and she
closed her eyes, her temples throbbing. She raised her
hand to massage her forehead.

"Let's step out for a breath of fresh air, Eric," she
said.

"You okay?"

"Sure, just a touch of a headache. It's stuffy in here,
don't you think?"

"No air circulating."

The band struck up again as they made their way
through the crowd to the entrance.

Outside, Kitty leaned against a parked car. She began telling Eric about Rick, not knowing why. He told
her about a woman he'd just broken up with. After a
while they went back inside.

Eric asked her to dance. "Sure, why not?" she said.

He grinned. "Watch out for my feet. I can't dance like Nate."

"I have a knack for stepping on arches myself," Kitty replied.

He laughed, and propelled her around the circle of dancers. Kitty felt unreasonable resentment toward Laurie but tried to contain it.

"You were going to tell us about the case Nate was working on," she said. "What really happened? You know—the shoot-out?" She tried to keep her voice light, but she was dying to hear the facts.

"Nate's so close-mouthed sometimes." Eric chewed down hard on a piece of gum. "Believe me, he's willing to do whatever it takes to get the job done."

She waited for him to go on. He didn't. A thin film of perspiration covered his face.

"When we were kids he never looked for trouble but he knew how to end it quickly enough if it happened," she prompted.

Eric nodded. "Nate works on some absorbing cases. Yeah, he's the perfect undercover cop. Part of it's because he doesn't look or dress like one. And he's not hard to talk to, as we already know. Still, he might appear to be easygoing on the surface, but he can be tougher than a rattler if called for. With his charm, the crooks don't see him as the fuzz until it's too late. Talk about cool—the word was invented for him. You'll never see him lose his temper like some cops, either. He's doggedly persistent to the point of . . . you know."

Kitty tried to sort out what Eric said. They had moved only a few steps in the crush of dancers. "No, I don't know. And the case you mentioned?"

"Naw. Let's forget it. No need riling our old friend Nate."

Kitty knew that much of Nate's life focused on the dark side of human nature. She could only guess at how dangerous his days and nights might be. "If you insist," she said, letting the subject drop.

All at once his breath felt hot on her cheek and the gum smelled too sweet. The music seemed overly loud. The thought of getting out of there was looking better all the time. She wanted to go home.

They came back to the table. Laurie and Nate had returned. Laurie's pretty face was inches from his. "Now, 'fess up," she said. "It was you who put the tack in our geometry teacher's chair."

Nate laughed. "I thought you did it."

Laurie giggled with delight. "You're so clever, and you didn't get those muscles working out in a gym once a week, I'll bet."

He lumbered to his feet and grinned. "You're putting me on."

He looked embarrassed, and turned, reaching out for Kitty. "Let's dance."

For a moment his eyes burned into hers with a magnetism that held her prisoner. Her skin felt on fire. She wasn't sure whether it was the effects of the heat in the room or the touch of his fingers drawing her out of the chair.

On the dance floor, Nate slipped his arm around Kitty's waist and took her hand, holding it close to his heart. His blue eyes glistened as his mouth formed a familiar smile.

The feel of his well-developed back muscles moving under her palm made her own heart quicken. Even through the fabric of his shirt, it was still touching him.

In his own way Nate was incensed with Kitty. For most of the evening she had acted standoffish, like they had never been close. He had listened to Laurie's endless chatter and it was giving him a migraine. She virtually leaned in to catch every phrase he uttered, and she wore too much makeup. Kitty was so different—more womanly. He admired her long shapely legs, her feminine curves, the way she swayed naturally when she moved into a fast dance step. The thought of her lovely attributes set his blood pumping overtime. She tilted her head back and tossed him a dazzling smile. Unable to resist, he brushed her temple with his lips, yearning to smother her mouth with kisses.

Blast that Rick Grant, whoever he was! Nate wished he could squeeze every thought of the guy out of her brain. She lowered her long eyelashes. He thought for a moment that he glimpsed a look of sadness. How he wished he could declare himself—make her listen while he poured out his love like cream in a mug of coffee. But he remembered his birthday party and their squabble.

This is absurd, he told himself. *What's going on with her?* His mouth tightened. While Laurie was throwing herself at him, Kitty was withdrawing. He knew how self-confident and full of fun Kitty could be. But now he sensed the tension in her body, those very limbs that he wanted to melt into his. Her reserve sobered him. Why did she keep saying she wanted a platonic relationship, when he wanted so much more?

Ease up, he told himself. "I haven't seen much of

you the last few days. Are you still going home for Christmas?"

"Yes. We'll be going to the Christmas ball at the country club. But you've probably forgotten about those stuffy affairs."

"I haven't forgotten. I suppose the town's 'four hundred' will be there." He gave her a jovial grin. "I'll probably pull duty, anyway. Me being a single guy."

"Mother always insists on going. You know, it's the town's big event."

The delicate scent of her perfume threatened to drive Nate to distraction. He dipped her back, then toward him to the steps of the music, the two of them moving in tandem. Then the music ended. She leaned into him, creating a powerful surge of electricity with the contact. He was reluctant to release her but she backed away.

"Kitty . . ."

She opened her mouth to speak, hesitated a moment, then blurted, "Rick's coming to the ball, too."

Nate folded his arms over his chest in outrage. "You're still thinking about him!"

Her glare matched his. "Yes!" Then all at once her features seemed on the verge of crumpling.

"Don't think you can turn me away that easily," he growled, his senses raw. "I'm a pretty determined guy."

She sighed heavily. "You're plain old stubborn."

"I'm stubborn? Look who's calling the kettle black!"

She smiled. "Okay, we're both stubborn."

When her fingers brushed the rough skin of his chin in an act of apology, it played havoc with his need all over again. He reached out and grasped her fingers, drawing them to his lips. She didn't fight him as he kissed their tips, his gaze locked on hers.

Then he released her hand, not uttering a word. A strange ringing rattled around in his ears as he stared into those soft blue eyes.

"We're not the same people, Kitty," he said quietly. "School's out. When are you going to realize that fact?"

"I'm beginning to," she murmured in honesty.

They returned to the table. Laurie and Eric weren't there.

"We need to talk, but not here." Nate's jaw worked. "Tomorrow night okay? Without Laurie."

"I promised to drive Olivia and Laurie to Palmella tomorrow. I won't be back until after the holidays."

Eric and Laurie, their arms around each other's waists, swayed up to the table, telling jokes and laughing.

Kitty smiled at them. "We really ought to be going, Laurie. It's getting late."

"So soon? I loved every minute of this glorious evening," Laurie said in her throaty, theatrical voice. She leaned over to kiss Nate full on the lips, but he turned his head and the kiss landed on his cheek.

Kitty tried not to be incensed with her friend, but right then she had the urge to strangle her. Nate uncoiled his long legs, getting to his feet. "Let me drive you girls home," he said.

"That's not necessary. But thanks anyway," Kitty said. "I have my car."

Laurie looked disappointed.

Later, sleep eluded Kitty. She lay in bed staring up at the dusky ceiling, trying to chase away the image of Nate and Laurie with their heads together. Her mouth tightened and she clasped her hands behind her head. Why had she acted like a jealous schoolgirl?

When sleep finally came, one of her worst nightmares beset her. She was looking down at her father in his casket. When she finally awoke in the wee hours, she curled up, hugging her knees, feeling terribly depressed.

The following morning Kitty came downstairs. Laurie was in the kitchen, sitting at the table.

"I'm on my second cup of coffee," Laurie said. "You must have really zonked out. It's after ten."

Kitty gave her a wan smile. "I don't usually sleep late." She poured herself a cup of coffee and joined Laurie.

Laurie nibbled on a croissant. "These are outstanding. Olivia said she makes them all the time. She's in the garden puttering around right now."

Kitty merely nodded. Olivia couldn't bake. The warmth of the coffee mug felt good in her palms. Laurie's eyes were red and swollen, and part of her hair was skewed to one side where she had slept on it. Kitty ran her finger absentmindedly around the rim of the mug and yawned, feeling lethargic.

"I haven't stayed out that late in a long time, and believe me, I know better. Always have to be on the set at the crack of dawn," Laurie said. Her unpainted lips reflected a grayish cast. "Got any cucumbers for my eyes?" She giggled. "I had a super time all the same. Those guys sure have changed. Too bad we can't do something exciting tonight with them."

Kitty groaned inwardly. Why had she picked a friend like Laurie? Laurie was beautiful, had the world's best figure, and attracted any man in a room.

Kitty, however, felt her own looks were ordinary and her hair wouldn't do what she wanted it to.

"I'm glad you had a good time," she said.

Kitty wished she had some comfort food, like her mom's key lime pie, to make her feel better. She glanced out the window at fan palms swaying softly in the breeze.

Laurie focused her full attention on Kitty, with a curious change of expression. "I don't care what you say, you *more* than like ol' Nate."

"But that's . . ." Her throat went dry.

"Ridiculous? That used to be one of your favorite words. Hello! You're the one being ridiculous. Why don't you tell him how you feel?" She grinned. "He's charming and confident, a self-possessed man. What woman wouldn't be attracted to him?"

Kitty straightened. "You're forgetting I like—love—Rick. Marriage to him would be safe. Besides, romance doesn't last. You're a blithe spirit, Laurie, you must know that. Look at all the divorces these days. Remember Dorothy Hinckle from back home? She's already gone that route."

"Get real! And who says romance doesn't last? Look at our folks. You're a fool if you don't forget about Rick. Nate's crazy about you."

"I could never marry anyone in law enforcement. Look what happened to my dad. It broke my mother's heart."

"But who's to say . . . ?"

Kitty changed the subject. "About last night. Call me a wet blanket. I don't know why I acted like such a snit, but I did have a headache—sort of."

Laurie gave her head a shake and her hair fell into place. "Oh, stop it, for heaven's sake. What a difference a few years make. Nate turned out to be such a good-looking guy, whereas Eric . . . Too many dough-nuts, I'm thinking." She grinned. "Now admit you care about Nate. I saw your eyes light up when we got there, and I also saw those darts you gave me. I was only being friendly."

Kitty gave her a wan smile and took a drink of coffee instead of replying.

"You were always good at keeping secrets, Kitty. Well, it's easy to see Nate's in love with you—and that's no secret, my friend. He listened politely to my babble, but I didn't pick up any vibes, even though I admit I tried hard enough. The vibes were all going in your direction, honeybun."

Kitty sat the cup down and formed a little church with her fingers, feeling foolishly inadequate.

Laurie took a nibble of croissant, then put the re-mainder on her dish. "Wake up, girl, before some other woman ensnares him."

"You haven't met Rick," Kitty reminded her. "He's really a nice guy."

Laurie sighed heavily. "I don't doubt it. But where *is* this jewel of a man?"

Kitty cleared her throat, and all of a sudden she felt sick inside. "I don't know what to say, Laurie. I think I've got an anxiety disorder coming on." She fumbled in her jeans pocket for a tissue.

"Next it'll be panic attacks." Laurie smiled imp-ishly. "Let not your heart be troubled, old girl, as it says in the Bible, or was it Shakespeare? Life was a whole lot simpler when we were kids." With a sym-pathetic pat of the hand, she rose to her feet. "Frankly, your talk about not being in love with Nate is pure baloney." She glanced down at her watch. "We better think of getting on the road pretty soon. It's going on eleven already."

Kitty felt better, but it didn't last long. She knew things in her personal life needed to be settled before she drove herself to distraction.

Chapter Seven

Kitty drove Laurie and Olivia to Palmella. She dropped off Laurie at her parents' house. She'd only just arrived at her mother's home, when she heard a car pull up in the driveway. A quick peek out the window told her Rick Grant had arrived. He unfolded himself from the car and glanced at the house, his hand shielding his eyes from the sun.

"Rick!" Kitty called out. She ran her hands through her hair. "I'll be right out!"

They embraced in the driveway. Rick's warm smile and light kiss reassured her. His dark brown hair was combed back from his pale square face and his brown eyes closed when he smiled. He was wearing a herringbone jacket and brown slacks.

"I'm glad you came," she said.

Rick stood back for a moment, scrutinizing her face. "I've missed you. We haven't been spending enough time together." His voice trailed off.

Unspoken questions teased the edges of her mind, but she would deal with them later.

"We're going to have a good time together." She fastened her arm through his. "Come in and meet my mom and my uncle."

"I have to fly out of here the night after Christmas. My parents insist. Haven't seen them in a year."

"The night after Christmas?" Astounded, she pulled her arm away. "That means we'll only have two days!" Had she been hoping to recapture something that was already lost?

"I know. I'm disappointed, too, but it can't be helped. Let's make every minute count. Come on, no sad faces."

Kitty grinned, trying to put her disappointment onto a back burner. Rick took a suitcase out of the car trunk and followed her into the house.

"Real nice of your mom to invite me to be her guest."

"She's looking forward to it."

In the living room, Kitty's uncle Joe pumped Rick's hand. "Glad to meet you, son."

Mary looked him over carefully. "We're happy to have you here, Rick."

Kitty introduced him to Olivia.

"How nice to meet you at last. Kit's so happy to have you join us."

Mary had put Olivia in the guest bedroom, and Joe was already occupying the other one.

"I hope you won't mind sleeping in the family room on the fold-out sofa," Mary said to Rick. "We seem to have run out of spare rooms."

"That will be fine."

Kitty saw his barely masked grimace, when her mother told him where he would sleep.

"I know we'll all enjoy the Christmas ball tomorrow night," Mary said.

Joe adjusted his slipping belt, pulled it up over the tire around his waist, and eyed Rick with a noncommittal gaze. *So much for the introductions,* Kitty thought.

The Christmas Eve ball was in full swing by the time they arrived. Kitty and Rick had come in his car. The brief drive was the first time she had been alone with him, except for last night's walk, when they had sauntered down to the swamp. His kiss had left her far from breathless. The mosquitoes were so thick that they spent most of the time swatting their arms and necks. In the end, they retreated to the house.

The ballroom looked festive. Red and green balloons and streamers hung from the ceiling. They found her mother's table and said their hellos. Then Rick took her aside.

"Your lace dress suits you," he murmured, holding her hand. "I like how the hem barely touches your ankles. You're very beautiful."

"You always did notice details. Thanks."

He led her to the dance floor. Kitty looked back over her shoulder at their little party. Olivia wore a tailored black sheath, her mother an emerald-green cocktail dress, the same one she had worn the year before. Joe looked distinguished in a black suit.

Rick and Kitty melted into the crowd of merrymakers. Most of them were dressed in black tie and sequins for Palmella's big event. Kitty waved to a few old acquaintances as the night progressed.

After a whirlwind of dancing, they started back to the table. Kitty fanned herself. Doc Thumb, her childhood doctor, came up and asked if she would honor him with a dance.

"Of course." She introduced him to Rick. They shook hands. The doctor took her gallantly in his arms and they swung out among the dancers.

"I haven't seen you since you had the flu that winter when we had a cold wave," he said. "Froze all the oranges."

"It's good to see you and all the familiar faces," Kitty said. "I saw Miss Lindley, my old chemistry teacher, over there by the band. She's the one who insisted I go to college."

"You've certainly come into your own, from what your mother says." He smiled indulgently. "I can't believe all you kids have grown up. Makes me feel downright old."

Kitty chuckled. But a sadness touched her heart when she noticed the filmy cataracts in his once-sharp blue eyes. He moved with a stiff arthritic gait. She was on the verge of asking him about his wife, when a hand landed gently on the old doctor's shoulder. She turned her head, expecting Rick, and met the penetrating gaze of Nate Mansfield about to cut in. His muscular frame filled out the well-cut tuxedo like few men could. She gasped.

"Dr. Thumb, I'm Nate Mansfield." He nodded courteously. "I believe you delivered me."

"Ah, yes," the doctor said. "You've grown a mite since then."

Nate laughed and Kitty found herself laughing, too, wondering how often the good doctor pulled that line.

He handed her over to Nate. "Take good care of

this young lady. She's about the prettiest girl here to-night."

Kitty thanked him and he sauntered away.

Nate's strong arm encircled her waist and he clasped her hand, nestling it close. "I'm shocked to see you," she said, her pulse rate increasing. His aftershave smelled pleasantly woodsy.

"You look gorgeous. But why are you so shocked?"

"You never mentioned you were coming to the dance, that's why."

"You didn't ask." His lips turned up in a smile. "Beautiful Kitty. Besides, my dear widowed Aunt Mildred asked me to be her escort. Anything wrong with that? Or was I supposed to stay away?"

"Of course nothing's wrong with your being here. I just wasn't expecting to see you. You mentioned working."

"They gave me time off for good behavior." He buried his face in her hair. She feared he'd feel the throbbing of her pulse. When she attempted to pull back, he held her fast, then eased up, the two of them moving in perfect rhythm to the music.

"I haven't seen you since the dance," he said, his voice soft. "You looked like you were ready to chew nails most of the evening. Don't tell me you're jealous of Laurie. Got to admit, she's turned into a beautiful woman." He chuckled.

"Jealous! How ridiculous. Whatever gave you such an absurd notion? You can be so infuriatingly cocksure of yourself, Nate."

He laughed at her with affection. "Because you're in love with me." His mouth twisted into a wide grin, while he made a fast turn to prevent them from careening into another couple. They nearly bumped noses.

"You're totally off base! Now quit holding me so tight. I can hardly breathe." His warm body so close to hers threatened to extinguish her righteous indignation.

"Darling, I'm hopelessly in love with you. Nothing you can say will alter that."

"What am I going to do with you?"

Nate shrugged. "You'll think of something."

Her eyes flickered beguilingly. She might seem to be speaking in a frank manner, but he believed she was holding back. He closed his eyes for a brief moment, and fought the urge to shake some sense into her. But he controlled the impulse. Kitty looked beautiful. He jealously wondered if she had worn the new lace dress especially to please that nerd. It didn't help his mood. However, he resolved to play Mr. Cool no matter what. Love was a risky business, he told himself, but so was life.

He forced his eyes away from hers, fearing he'd get lost in their depths. He glanced at the tall Christmas tree in the center of the room. Then he spotted Mary, Kitty's mother, talking to a bookish-looking man near the table laden with hors d'oeuvres. He had seen the man come in with Kitty earlier. Rick Grant. He wasn't impressed.

"Give me time to think," Kitty said, cutting into his thoughts. "I need a little space."

Nate didn't reply. When the music ended, and he let her go, Kitty hurried to join Mary and Rick. Having Nate so close left her trembling. Rick took both of her hands and stepped back to observe her. "I swear you get more beautiful all the time, Kitty. Doesn't she, Mrs. O'Hara?"

Mary cooed, "Oh, yes," and smiled with pride.

"Thank you." Kitty was determined not to glance back to see if Nate stood there watching them.

Mary gave Kitty a fond smile and went back to their table. The night had quickly slipped into a quagmire, Kitty thought, worse than the western dance. How dare Nate show up without so much as a hint! She found herself on the verge of tears, and wondered at herself. She wasn't usually given to histrionics. But seeing Nate so unexpectedly brought on powerful emotions— feelings she desperately tried to keep submerged.

Laurie arrived with an entourage of family members.

"Kitty, here you are! And who's this?" She turned to Rick, a glamor-shot of a smile on her beautiful face. Her short, tight, black dress showed off her exceptional figure. Kitty suddenly felt like a frump.

A broad grin worked its way over Rick's face. "Kitty, introduce me."

"This is my friend, Laurie. I told you about her. We went to high school together."

"I call Hollywood home now," Laurie added. "I'm an actress." She tossed her mane of blond hair.

Rick's eyes widened with interest. He turned his back on Kitty and asked Laurie a question about movie-making. Laurie's interest swelled as she related some of her experiences. Kitty felt like a fifth wheel.

"I've been dying to meet you, Rick." Laurie inched her way close to him, fogging his glasses. "Kitty says you've nearly finished your internship. I find intelligent men so intriguing."

"Oh?" He grinned. "Would you like to dance with this intriguing man?"

Laurie threw Kitty a conspiratorial smile. "All right with you?"

Kitty nodded, knowing she had been upstaged. Laurie looked every inch a movie star in her theatrical makeup and platform high heels. They made her shapely legs look like a Las Vegas showgirl's.

Rick raised his brows to Kitty, a little apologetic, and led Laurie to the dance floor. Kitty stood watching them. He seemed mesmerized by Laurie. A twinge of jealousy hit Kitty once more, but it was barely a twinge.

Mary patted the seat next to her. "Sit down, Kitty." She had apparently been observing them, too. "Laurie's certainly changed. But she always did command a lot of attention. I think I'll go say hello to her folks in a little while."

"Laurie's always had her pick of fellows, even in high school."

Funny, Nate didn't seem overwhelmed by her, Kitty thought, or maybe he was just clever enough to hide it. Joe, Kitty's uncle, poured her a glass of mineral water. She thanked him and took a sip, letting it refresh her.

In a little while Rick came back. He tried to mask his enjoyment but it stood out on his face like a coat of red paint.

"Phew! Your friend, Laurie, is a good dancer," he said. "Full of energy. Was she always so dynamic?"

"She was," Kitty replied. Rick's words irritated her. She would have preferred he use a different adjective—like pushy. But then, Laurie couldn't help being beautiful and fun-loving. Men were naturally entranced by her.

Rick stood up. "Why don't we dance?"

Although a bit miffed, Kitty didn't hesitate, and they made their way to the dance floor. When he held her against him she moved back a step. He tried to make eye contact but she looked the other way, aware of her childishness but not caring.

"Having a good time?" he asked.

"Splendid." She knew her voice sounded flat, but she thought it was a stupid question.

They danced in silence. Then her uncle cut in. Kitty welcomed Joe like a long-lost friend. Rick reluctantly let her go.

"Nice ball," Joe said, taking her hand. He was of medium height, with a thick shock of white hair that gave him a distinguished appearance.

"I'm glad you could come, Uncle Joe. I don't think I've seen you in nearly a year."

"Two's more like it."

"Oh? Where's the time go?"

"I ask myself that every day."

When the music stopped, he was about to take her back to the table when Nate appeared beside him.

"Hello, Joe," he said, shaking the older man's hand. "Remember me? Nate Mansfield. I used to live next door to Kitty."

"What a pleasure to see you again." Joe patted him on the back. "Come on over to the table and join us. Mary will be delighted to see you. Tell me how your folks are doing. I moved away from Palmella several years ago after my wife died. Live in one of those retirement places. Not too bad."

"My parents are fine. They also moved. And thanks for the invitation. I will."

Kitty swallowed with difficulty. Things weren't going as she planned. They followed Joe back to the table. Olivia glanced up, her thin lips parting with pleasure.

"Nate," she said. "How nice to see you. I'm quite surprised."

Nate smiled. "Good to see you, ma'am." He slipped into a seat beside Olivia and they put their heads together for a tête-à-tête. Mary came back from visiting with Laurie's family and hugged him affectionately. A long conversation followed. Kitty was on pins and needles. She wished he'd go before Rick came back. How could she have gotten herself into such a mess?

Rick returned. She wondered if he had been dancing with Laurie again. Introductions followed. The two men eyed each other warily and shook hands. Nate, tall and broad-chested, a little rough around the edges, and Rick, the academic one, had finally met.

"Nate and I grew up together," Kitty told Rick. "He's like, uh, a brother." She noted Nate's slight grimace.

Rick asked Kitty to dance. When he took her elbow and they drifted off, she felt Nate's eyes boring into her back.

Nate didn't like seeing Kitty dance cheek-to-cheek with the nerd. He sat there seething and tried not to show it. The music was devilishly slow. As though an antenna had sprouted on the top of his head, he didn't lose sight of them as they moved in and out among the dancers.

He hadn't liked the smile Kitty gave Rick when he

asked her to dance. Frustrated, Nate asked Olivia if she'd like to dance. She agreed. On the floor he carried on an interesting conversation with the matron, but that wasn't too difficult with Olivia. Then he caught sight of Kitty and Rick when he peered over Olivia's shoulder. Kitty was laughing at something Rick said.

Bitter, Nate made himself concentrate on his partner. However, all the while he was thinking that this was the man Kitty said she wanted to marry. No way! It wasn't going to happen if he could prevent it. The sight of her in Rick's arms made him burn with resentment.

"Are you having a good time?" Olivia asked.

For a brief moment he had almost forgotten who he was dancing with. "Sure. And you?"

"Oh, I'm having a very pleasant time. Kitty looks beautiful tonight, don't you think?"

He hesitated a moment. "Yeah. You look great, too."

She gave him a light, flirtatious grin. "You say the most agreeable things. That's why I like you. And I'm sure that's why Kitty likes you, too."

His interest picked up, but he didn't question her. The music was winding down. Kitty would soon be free to dance with him. He glanced over to where his Aunt Mildred sat at a table across the room. A couple of old friends were chatting with her. He doubted she'd think he was ignoring her.

When Nate brought Olivia back, she thanked him and he said, "The pleasure was all mine."

He danced with Mary next.

"Why don't you ask Mildred to join our little party?" she asked.

"The Higginses are with her now, but thanks, I will."

When he brought Mary back, Kitty and Rick still hadn't returned. He scanned the crowd while he went to find his aunt. Kitty apparently didn't miss him, and the realization hurt. Then he saw them standing off to the side of the dance floor. Kitty's face wasn't a foot away from Rick's, her head tilted forward as she listened to something he said. They seemed conscious only of each other. Rick laughed, then Kitty laughed in response, placing a finger to her mouth. Rick took her hand and she moved into his close embrace as they began to dance.

Jealousy rose in Nate's throat, nearly choking him. He could take no more. He'd had enough for one night of seeing Kitty in another man's arms. Depressed, he turned away. Maybe Mildred wanted to leave. She wasn't one for staying up much after 9:00, and it was already going on 11:00.

While they danced, Rick said, "Let's get out of here and go back to your place. You promised me some time to ourselves. Your family and friends are just great but I'm dying to kiss you without our putting on a floor show for the others." His eyes glinted.

"Let's." Kitty had been ready to go for ages. She had important things to say to him. There wasn't any use in putting it off any longer.

When they rejoined the others she was grateful Nate had finally disappeared. Having his gaze on her all evening had made her nervous. They said hasty good-byes to Olivia, Mary, and Joe, and hurried to the car. Rick opened the door. But before she could slide in, he took her in his arms and covered her lips with his.

She was swept away for a brief moment, the old magic flaring up between them. But then it died.

"Thank heavens we're finally alone," he said, his voice eager.

Kitty smiled, and slid in the car, wondering why she no longer felt eager herself.

When he started the engine, he shot her an appraising glance. "You seem preoccupied."

Kitty didn't reply, nor did she snuggle up to him, as she would have in the past.

"Turn to the left at the next stop sign," she said, when they pulled out of the parking lot.

Uncertainties and misgivings plagued her. She and Rick were already a universe apart. Her thoughts raced on. Why couldn't Nate have chosen to be a plumber or a schoolteacher, anything but a cop?

Rick drove down the dark country road. The car bumped, followed by a series of bigger bumps. He swore and pulled off the road onto the shoulder.

"What's the matter?" she asked, even though she was pretty sure what had happened.

"A darn flat. That's all we need."

He opened the door and got out, grumbling. A car came up behind them and stopped. Kitty made out the figure of a man approaching the car, raising her anxiety level. They were on a road seldom used. Would they be robbed—or worse? She slunk down.

The man called, "Need some help?"

Nate's voice! She bolted up and attempted to open the electric window but the ignition was off.

"Looks like you've picked up a nail or something," Nate said to Rick.

"Glad you came along. Nate, isn't it? I'd hate to be

stuck out on this lonely road all night. I've made other plans." He glanced back inside the car.

Nate whistled. "All the gas stations are closed by now. I don't suppose you want to change a tire in your tuxedo. I know I don't." He loosened his tie. "Let me give you a ride home. That's the least I can do. I've got my aunt's Cadillac. The old boat'll carry us all and then some."

Kitty threw open the door, stepped out into the darkness, and stumbled.

"Just what . . . ?" she exploded.

Nate caught her. She jerked away.

"Ah, Kitty O'Hara, what a surprise!"

"Surprise, is it?"

Common sense told her that this was no coincidence. Would Nate stoop so low as to give Rick's car a flat? But how would he know which one was Rick's? Then again, cops knew everything, didn't they?

Kitty and Rick piled into the back seat of Nate's aunt's car.

Mildred turned her head to welcome them and stifled a yawn. "I'm so sleepy. I hope I haven't spoiled the evening for Nate."

"No problem, Aunt Mildred." He put the car into gear.

Nate took the long way home. He dropped his aunt off first and saw to it she was comfortably settled. By the time they pulled into Mary O'Hara's driveway, it was nearly time for the ball to end. Kitty shot him a frosty thanks as she climbed out of the Cadillac.

"Aren't you going to invite me in for a cup of coffee?" he asked, his manner casual. "I might fall asleep on the way back to Mildred's."

Kitty was about to say, "Not on your life," when

Rick said, "How impolite of us not to think of it first. Come in."

Nate killed the engine and got out. He followed them into the living room, slouched in a chair, and made himself at home. Rick took off his glasses and rubbed his eyes. Kitty walked stiffly to the kitchen. She took the coffee canister out of a cupboard and accidentally tipped it over. Half of the contents fanned out on the floor like a pyramid. Grumbling, she scooped it into the coffeepot. The floor couldn't have too many germs since her mother was Mrs. Clean. She added water and turned on the switch, then mopped up the residue with a wet paper towel.

By the time the coffee was ready, and she had poured the steaming liquid into mugs, the commotion outside told her that her mother and the others had returned. Muttering, she took down more mugs and filled them. Somehow, she and Rick were not destined to spend time alone. He would be furious. But when she returned to the living room with a tray, the two men were in the midst of a deep conversation about the Miami Dolphins.

Kitty awoke the following morning, choking in quicksand, her heart pounding. She sat up and realized she was in her old bed. A cold sweat covered her. Nightmares—how she hated them.

The familiar sounds of the Irish Chieftains' music came from the living room, soothing her with the band's mixture of pipes, whistles, flutes, violins, accordions, harps, and drums. She got up, took a reviving shower, then slipped into denim jeans.

When Kitty came into the kitchen, her mother was

flipping pancakes. Nate looked up from the stack he was eating and threw her an impish grin.

"Hi. Your mom invited me over for breakfast. Just like old times. She always was the best cook in town." He looked quite refreshed in a sweatshirt and faded jeans.

Kitty bit a hangnail and shot him a withering look. It wasn't like her to have an attack of nerves. But this was too much! How dare he insert himself into her life when Rick was here!

Then she realized they were all staring at her. The spasm of irritation she felt must be showing on her face. She immediately wiped it away and forced a smile. Mary frowned, and was about to ask her something, but apparently decided against it. Uncle Joe darted a questioning glance over his reading glasses, then returned to the morning newspaper. Olivia said, "Good morning, dear." Then she took a sip of coffee. Rick sat up straighter, his gaze gliding from Kitty to Nate.

Kitty cleared her throat. "Good morning, everyone." She didn't meet Nate's eyes. He could play his little "boy-next-door" game if he wanted. Addressing Rick, she asked, "Did you sleep well?"

"Yes." His reply sounded halfhearted. Then he gave her a broad smile, showing his capped teeth. "And you?"

"Fine—just fine."

After breakfast, Nate thanked Mary, said his good-byes, and turned to Kitty. "By the way, I left you a little something for Christmas on your bedside table."

Kitty was astonished. She hadn't seen it. "Why, thanks, Nate." But then, that meant he must have sneaked into her room while she was in the shower.

"Go open it, dear," Mary said. "Let's see what he brought you. Maybe it's one of those little wooden birds he used to whittle."

Nate smiled. "It's nothing much. She can show it to you later."

He took his leave.

Outside, Nate flexed his fingers a couple of times and got in the Jeep. He had been so flustered that morning that he had put on two different-colored socks before his aunt caught the mistake. Why did Kitty have to be so petulant? She aggravated the tar out of him. What could she possibly see in that soft-bellied nerd? And here Nate was, living like a monk. But he knew the answer all too well. No other woman affected him like Kitty O'Hara, and she was worth the wait.

His moods changed directions faster than a tornado when he backed out of the driveway. But at least he hadn't let her shut him out. He only wished she needed him as much as he needed her.

Talking to himself, he mumbled in fury as he drove down the avenue toward the freeway. His love for Kitty caused him pure misery sometimes. Nate couldn't remember any other woman having that effect on him. Why didn't he just exorcise her from his brain? What kind of an idiot was he! *Face facts! She's in love with that guy.*

His bumper sticker read, *"Trespassers will be eaten alive,"* and a caricature of a pit bull glowered. It was just how his gut was feeling after putting on that asinine "happy-face" all morning.

Get a grip! he told himself. *Don't be stupid. Go home and jog for a while.*

Kitty continued to possess his thoughts as he turned

onto the freeway and headed back toward Miami. All he could think about was the satiny curve of her spine when he held her in his arms at the ball. "I'll grow a mustache," he muttered brusquely, when he finally reached his own driveway. Anything to make her see him different from that kid he used to be.

Kitty unwrapped Nate's gift, folded back the box's tissue paper, then let out her breath. Thank goodness she hadn't opened the gift at the kitchen table in front of everyone. No! No one would see this but her. She drew out a beautiful crocheted bikini from the finest swimwear boutique in Miami, a reminder of their day together at the beach. She grinned. How could she keep such a gift? "Nate Mansfield—what am I going to do with you!" Those words were fast becoming a regular part of her vocabulary.

Chapter Eight

When Kitty walked with Rick to his car, he took her in his arms and promised that they would soon be able to spend more time together. "I'll call you tonight."

He had given her a lovely amber pin for Christmas and she had given him a leather doctor's bag.

"We'll get reacquainted when I get back," he said. "As though we needed to do that!"

Kitty smiled weakly when he brushed a kiss against her cheek. "Hope you have a nice visit with your family."

She gave him a little wave as he drove away. Nothing had been resolved. She hadn't had a chance to bring up the subject of breaking off their relationship. He'd talked about wanting to be alone with her but he didn't demand it like Nate would have.

She was confident Nate had only come to the ball to keep his eye on her. The thought made her grin, now that it was all over. What a contrast the two of them made—one filled with fire and impulsiveness, the other practical and studious.

Rick didn't telephone Kitty that night. However, Nate did. "Just wanted to be sure you got back to the city all right," he said. "Traffic's getting awful."

It was good to know he cared. She had already put aside her irritation with him for not telling her he planned to show up at the ball. "It's only a sixty-mile drive," she said. "How are you? And thanks for the gift, although I shouldn't keep it."

"Why?"

"You know."

He let her implication go by. "Glad you liked it. I can hardly wait to see you model it."

"Nate!"

"Just kidding." He changed the subject. "That was some ball. You were the best part of the whole affair."

Kitty didn't speak for a moment but let the words bathe her. "I'm glad you came, even if you did give me a shock. I have a gift for you, too."

"Great. I had the feeling you didn't care, one way or the other, if I came."

"I'm sorry if I sounded rude."

He paused. "I'll be honest with you. I wanted to look Rick Grant over. And you know what I saw?"

"I'm almost afraid to ask. Okay, what?" she asked warily.

"A nice-enough guy. Sort of boring. But he'd never be enough for you."

Kitty raised her voice an octave. "What do you mean by that—not enough for me?" She tried to envision a safe marriage to Rick, but all of a sudden it seemed empty.

"You need a guy like me."

She started to laugh derisively but couldn't. Nate's words stirred in her mind like a boiling caldron. But she wasn't going to let him know just how on target he might be, if it wasn't for that one obstacle. "Nate, you know how I feel about your work."

"Your mother doesn't think it's so bad."

"And look what happened to her. Widowed."

Andrea Webster called Kitty into the office just as she was about to leave for the day. The woman pulled a notepad from the top drawer of her desk and jotted down something, then set the pen down.

"I'm so glad I caught you before you left," Andrea said. "I wanted to tell you how much I enjoy using your creams and lotions—especially the magnolia-scented night cream. It has such a divinely subtle fragrance." Her eyes flickered and her mouth turned up.

"Thanks," Kitty said. "I'm glad. Does that mean you're willing to use them here in the shop?"

"Well, yes, I think so. But since I'll be doing you a favor, I thought you might be willing to help me out." She smiled as though they had become close friends.

Kitty tried to hide her skepticism. Just what did Andrea have in mind?

"My nephew, Derek, flew in from New York last night. A delightfully funny fellow. I wanted to take him to dinner tonight but I'm all tied up. He's always been my favorite nephew." She acted girlish, quite out of character. "Could you go in my place, just this one time? I'd make it worth your while. In fact, I'll put

your line of cosmetics right up in front by the reception-
tionist desk. You'd like that, wouldn't you?"

Kitty was flabbergasted, and for a moment she
didn't know what to reply. Andrea's offer sounded
wonderful but also like bribery. Yet she indicated it
was a simple business arrangement. The thought of
having her cosmetics on display where clients were
bound to see them made her decision easy.

"Sure," Kitty said. "Where do you want me to take
him?"

"Fabulous! He's been to Miami before. I'll let him
decide. What a load off my mind. The poor darling.
He'll pick you up, say seven-thirty?"

Kitty nodded. It seemed innocent enough, even if it
wasn't something she was looking forward to. One
dinner, then she'd never have to see him again.

Nate called Kitty when she got home from work.

"How about catching a movie tonight?" he asked.

"I wish I could say yes but I'm taking Andrea's
nephew to dinner. Purely business. He's in town and
she can't get away. Sorry."

"Will you call me when you get back?"

"Gosh, I don't know how long it'll take. We're not
going until seven-thirty."

"I'll wait for your call. The time doesn't matter."

Nate placed the receiver back in its cradle. He idly
slipped his hands in his pockets and sauntered into the
kitchen. Poking around in the refrigerator, he guessed
a TV dinner was better than nothing.

So Kitty's boss had gotten her tied up with some
dude. Nate was already jealous of the time the guy
would take away from him. Outside, the weather

looked bleaker by the minute. He stood at the window, feeling gloomy. His big dog nuzzled his leg and he bent down to pet him.

He decided to sit down and write Kitty a love letter, calling himself a crazy, romantic jerk.

By 6:00, he hadn't committed one word to paper, although words were rolling around in his head. He stared at the telephone. His emotions were in a brooding turmoil. How was he to get Rick Grant out of Kitty's system? She could be so stubborn. But this was love. He'd known it after only one evening with her. There had been other women in his life but nothing serious. His work had taken priority, and most women couldn't adjust to that. No one but Kitty could make him want to live any other way. She was devastatingly beautiful, clever, and sweet. It was all he could do not to call her on the phone again. But she was going out with the boss's nephew. Why hadn't he thought to ask how old the guy was? Maybe this nephew was no more than twelve. But then, he could be thirty, for all he knew. Andrea was no spring chicken.

Nate leaned back. He could almost feel the fineness of Kitty's skin, see her expressive eyes glowing warmly at him. The thoughts made him ache with longing. His mood swung like a yo-yo between elation and despair.

He jotted a few words down, then wadded up the paper and threw it in the wastebasket. Taking another sheet, he composed a short letter, filling it with his deepest thoughts—then tossed it. He made several drafts before settling on one.

When he had finished, he stamped it, pulled on his windbreaker, and headed for his Jeep to mail it while he still had the courage.

* * *

Derek Long arrived promptly at 7:30. Olivia was chatting with him in the library when Kitty came downstairs. Kitty had chosen a gray suit with a white silk blouse, wanting to keep a professional look.

Derek was of medium height and a bit on the heavy side, his hairline slightly receding. But he looked pleasant enough, Kitty thought. He had been gazing past Olivia at the Van Gogh over the desk.

"Very impressive," he said after the introductions, turning back to the artwork.

He seemed more interested in the painting than in Kitty, and for that she was grateful. When he went on about art, she smiled, suspecting Olivia's original paintings had been sold long ago. If anyone would know where to find a good fake, it would be Olivia. She was a clever lady, living in style even if it had to be fabricated.

When they said good-bye to her and went outdoors, the wind whipped Kitty's hair and she reached up to try to repair the damage. Derek opened the car door for her. It was a rented Toyota. She climbed in, asking herself why she had agreed to do this.

They drove to a hotel in Miami Beach with an ocean view. Kitty noticed the surf churning black. Angry, thick clouds formed as darkness descended. Hurricane? She put the notion out of her mind. It wasn't the season.

A slim hostess led them to an excellent table by a window. The tables were partly sectioned off by potted palms.

"Andrea says this place has great food," Derek said. He scanned the room over the potted palms. "But you've probably been here, before, anyway."

Kitty shook her head. "No. I haven't, but it looks very nice."

When a waiter came Derek ordered a drink. She asked for Perrier. He looked disappointed.

"I'm actually from New Jersey." He leaned forward, his abdomen bulging slightly with the effort, and took out a package of cigarettes, lighting one. "Cigarette?" he offered. She declined. He took a deep draw, like a man taking his last breath.

Kitty hated the thought of spending the evening surrounded by swirling smoke. *Just one night,* she reminded herself. A tiny gap between his shirt buttons revealed pale skin. He was heavier than he appeared when he'd stood in Olivia's library.

"Do you come to Florida often?" she asked, making conversation.

"Often enough. Finding a doll like you is going to make the trips a lot more palatable." He grinned with a playful, roguish air. "I work for a big brokerage firm on Wall Street." He threw his shoulders back, registering his importance.

"I'm afraid I don't know much about the market," she said.

He pursed his mouth. Kitty figured by his expression he probably thought she was a country hick.

The waiter came with drinks. It had begun to rain— hard, furious rain. The distracting sounds of window-panes rattling unsettled her, along with the blackness outside.

"Looks like a tropical storm's moved in," she said.

Derek ignored her remark. He took a sizable gulp of his drink and smacked his lips. "Outstanding! But you haven't tried yours." He snuffed his cigarette in an ashtray and lit another.

"It's fine," Kitty answered coolly.

He gazed at her, his eyes traveling in a downward motion to cover her. Then he looked up, apparently pleased by what he saw. "Andrea says you're in the cosmetics business. Are you listed on the stock exchange?"

"No." She laughed at the absurdity of his question, raising her hand to her throat. "My business is very small scale."

"You're awfully young to be in business at all. But I have to tell you I admire ambitious women. I'm planning to be a millionaire myself by the time I reach my mid-thirties. I'll still be young enough to enjoy it, wouldn't you say? Maybe move to the Cayman Islands. Great tax shelters there." Then, as an afterthought, he added, "I play the commodities. It can be cutthroat but lucrative for those willing to gamble."

"Oh," Kitty replied. She had only a vague idea of what commodities were. "Living on an island sounds nice."

The waiter came to take their orders. Kitty was about to say, "I'll have the sautéed shrimps and scallops," when Derek ordered Chateaubriand for two with all the trimmings. Kitty didn't even know what it was, but she figured he was trying to impress her.

"And bring us another round," he said when the waiter was about to put down his pencil. Derek ground the butt of his cigarette into the ashtray and lit another.

Kitty's irritation was getting harder to reign in, and her eyes stung. She took out a tissue and dabbed.

Derek proceeded to talk nonstop about his work and people she didn't know, until the waiter returned. She tried to act interested, even though boredom had long since set in. His mannerisms put Kitty on edge, and when he smacked his lips, she glanced away in disgust. She fidgeted in the seat, and took a quick peek at her watch. Had they been there only a half hour?

"I did some investing for Andrea a while back," Derek said, with a conspiratorial glance around the room. "Did all right, too. Put her on easy street for the rest of her life." Then he bragged about how successful he was.

"Ah," Kitty said. "Now I know why Andrea considers you to be such a darling."

Derek laughed heartily. "I might be able to do the same for you, when we get to know each other better, that is."

"I don't think I'm anywhere near ready to invest."

The waiter brought green salads, along with a basket of Italian rolls. It looked like a meal all by itself. Kitty speared a leaf and took a bite, leaving the bread alone. When she looked up, Derek had consumed most of his salad and was stuffing a roll in his mouth. His cigarette burned in the ashtray, the smoke spiraling in her direction. She reached over and put it out.

"Good food!" He swallowed hard and reached for another roll.

Kitty thought that all he needed was an apple in his mouth and he'd look like a stuffed pig.

The waiter brought a large sizzling steak on a plank. He arranged the dinner plates and various side dishes. Derek's eyes practically bugged open with anticipation. So this was Andrea's dear nephew? Kitty wished she'd never met either of them.

"Bring more rolls," he told the waiter.

The poker-faced man nodded and disappeared.

Sighing, Kitty picked up her knife and fork, thinking there was enough beef on her plate to feed a family. Her appetite evaporated with the thought.

Derek ate with a vengeance, while Kitty tried not to watch. She was on the verge of shouting, "This is an almighty disaster!" but she kept her cool.

When the busboy took away her nearly full plate, Derek didn't seem to notice.

"How about a nightcap, Kit?" he asked, lighting a cigarette with satisfaction.

"I've really got to go," she declared, and got to her feet. Enough was enough!

He shrugged, and paid the bill. They headed for the heavy glass entrance door. When he opened it, a gust of wind nearly blew both of them backward into the lobby.

"What a gale!" he said, the wind carrying his words away.

Once outside, they fought the wind. Kitty's skirt clung to her legs as they headed for the parking garage.

Before he opened the car door, he grabbed her and gave her a slobbery kiss. She yanked free. The temptation to bop him with her purse was almost overpowering. He laughed, as though she had told him a funny joke, and reached for her again, making kissing sounds.

"Come here," he yelled.

Kitty, on the verge of gagging, wrenched away and screeched, "I'd rather kiss a pig!"

"Feisty," he roared.

"Good night!" She turned and looked around, hoping to see a cab near the entrance. He grabbed her from the back. She gave him a strong elbow in the ribcage and he growled in pain and released her. No way was she going to ride home with this octopus.

Kitty left Derek standing by his car and hurried from the parking garage. Outside, palm trees took on an eerie life of their own as they gyrated wildly in the storm. The wind whipped her hair about her face. Her first thought was to find a telephone and call Olivia, but then she rejected it. The widow was afraid to drive at night, and the weather had turned ugly. A quick glance told her no cabs were parked in front of the restaurant.

Kitty tucked her purse under her arm and moved with precarious steps on down the street, hoping she'd spot one soon. She could hear the waves pounding fiercely against the beach on the other side of the buildings. The storm seemed as devastating as a hurricane. The rain came down in gray sheets. All she could think about was finding cover.

Chapter Eight

Battling her way through the growing maelstrom, drenched, her suit ruined, Kitty came to a streetcorner. She tried to make a decision whether to go back to the restaurant or walk a little farther on. A roof tile dropped with a thud not more than a foot from her. Gasping, she hugged the wall of the building, then turned back and inched along. A palm frond swished overhead like a giant predatory bird and careened into the wall up ahead. The sidewalk was so slippery she had to fight to keep her balance. The sound of the sea thundered in her ears.

"This is madness!" she cried out, terrified, her hair matted to her scalp.

She had to take cover. Just then a gray seagull hurled against a nearby windowpane, bursting through it like a bomb. Glass flew everywhere, barely missing her. Something slimy splashed onto her forehead. When she scraped it off, it turned out to be a petunia.

Across the street a palm tree was partly uprooted, resembling the Leaning Tower of Pisa.

It seemed like hours since she foolishly left the parking garage, although it was only a block away. Coming to a doorway, she huddled in its alcove to catch her breath. The driving rain came down with such force that it was hard to see.

What am I going to do? she asked herself, the terror inside her mounting. Just then, she spotted a cab as it turned the corner, and she lunged forward to flag it down.

Nate watched the barometer tumble. All afternoon suspicious thunderstorm clusters were being reported from the Caribbean, along with a falling atmospheric pressure over the gulf. The air was heavy. By 9:00 the winds topped sixty miles an hour. The hurricane, though out of season, appeared to be swinging ashore. The National Hurricane Center hadn't forecasted the tropical storm to turn into a hurricane, but here it was in full force.

Nate worried about Kitty.

Thinking she might have called off the dinner date, he telephoned. Mrs. Christenson told him where they had gone. Good ol' Olivia! He headed over that way at about the time he figured Kitty and her dinner date would be finishing. He told himself he wasn't stalking her—something he swore he'd never do. But by heaven, he wanted to get a look at the guy. The undercover cop in him was on the scent. All he needed was a bloodhound and Sherlock Holmes's funny-looking cap, he told himself with a rueful grin.

Nate didn't have to wait long. He recognized her coming out with some big-shouldered ex-football player type with a thick neck. And even in the rain, he could see the guy's muscles had turned to flab. Nate witnessed the confrontation between them, and his anger whipped to the boiling point. He was about to drive into the parking garage and twist the guy's arm behind his back, when Kitty pulled away and started off down the street. She didn't see his Jeep parked close by. He ought to rescue her then and there. Yet Nate knew that if he showed up like Sir Galahad, she'd guess he'd followed her and be plenty angry.

All right, he told himself. *Be cool. Just see what happens next. Maybe she'll hail a cab.* But there didn't seem to be any around. Now what was he going to do? If he simply hopped out of Jeep and offered her a ride, she'd probably explode, especially after the ball.

Nate let her continue down the street, reasoning that by the time she was a block into this mayhem, she'd be glad to see anyone—even him.

When he saw Kitty hover like a drenched rabbit in a doorway, he figured enough was enough. He pulled over to the curb, and was opening the door, when she stepped out, slipped, and slid into the street. A cab sped by, barely missed her, and spread a shower of dirty water. With his heart pumping overtime, he shrugged off the wet assault and dashed to her side.

"Kitty, darling," he shouted above the wind, "you hurt?" He cradled her in his arms, then swooped her up and ran back to his car.

"Nate!" Surprise registered on her face as she clung to him. "How'd you get here?" She paused. "I'm okay, I think."

He didn't reply as he put her in the Jeep and closed the door, his throat constricting. She could have been killed! What an idiot he'd been. Beside him in the car, she huddled, wet and bedraggled, as he drove carefully down the avenue.

They reached the Christenson house and he took her key and unlocked the entrance door. The wind howled, nearly blowing them through the threshold. Kitty coughed. "Nate?"

"Yes, darling?"

"I'm freezing. And I need a hot bath. But thanks for being there for me."

"Do you want help?"

She hesitated. "It frightens me so much."

"What frightens you, Kitty?"

"Loving you."

She turned and fled upstairs. He stood there, astonished, his mouth open. Did he hear right? Did she admit she loved him? His chest expanded as his heart soared.

Nate waited in the library for Kitty to come back downstairs.

After she had showered and put on a white terry-cloth robe, they sat across from each other in the library. Nate had made coffee. He handed Kitty a cup. The widow must have gone to bed hours ago.

"How did you find me?" She held the cup so that the steam touched her face.

"Uh, I called here. Olivia told me you'd gone to that restaurant. Guess I'd forgotten you told me you were going out. I was passing by on my way home from the post office when I thought I saw you. What were you doing out there alone?" He kept quiet about seeing her with the man.

Her eyes rounded. "What a coincidence. Wasn't that a long way from the post office?"

Here it comes, Nate told himself with a straight face. *Nothing comes easy.* He thought he'd turn the questions in her direction, but she was too quick for him.

She shot him an amused grin. "You just happened to be passing by in this big city and recognized me in that deluge?"

He raised a hand, hating himself for lying. "Scout's honor."

She didn't look as though she bought it. He picked up her bare foot and began to gently massage it. Her robe parted, exposing an enticingly shapely knee. Then he saw the abrasion an inch or two below.

"Cut yourself, did you?" He almost reached over to kiss it.

She covered her leg. "Nothing bad."

"I'll get you a Band-Aid."

"No need. I'm eternally grateful you came along. But if I thought you were following me . . . well, I would find that completely intolerable. I can certainly take care of myself."

He grinned, ignoring the reprimand. "The storm's still raging. Maybe I ought to put a stake through its heart."

Kitty laughed.

He stood up. "If we're lucky it'll blow back out to sea. Got to be going. You get some sleep."

"Well, were you?" she said.

"Was I what?" He spread his hands in a gesture that said he was innocent. Then he leaned down and brushed a kiss against her damp hair.

"There's another thing I've been dying to ask you,"

she said. "Tell the truth now. Did you do something to Rick's tire at the Christmas ball?"

"No. I'd never do that," and he meant it. "But I figured you thought I did. I decided to leave when I saw you go out. No point in my staying, and my aunt complained of being tired. I was there when you pulled away and thought I noticed the tire looked low. Well, what was I supposed to do? I followed just to make sure you got home safe. I'm a cop. I do things like that." He winked.

She smiled, as though she still didn't entirely believe him.

"You shouldn't go out in that storm. Stay here. Olivia has plenty of rooms."

"Can't. I'm on call."

"But I'll be worried about you."

"Don't do that." He hesitated a moment, then grinned. "See you around, kid." He kissed her cheek, then reluctantly left her there alone.

"Where were you, Kit?" Olivia asked the next afternoon. She reclined in a lounge chair on the terrace. "I haven't seen you all day."

"Working on a new formula. Then I went for a walk on the beach, trying to sort out some new turns in my life."

"Sometimes I'm not always tactful, but I must say I believe you're thinking too much. Just follow your heart, my dear. Don't try to analyze everything. You can't really choose who you're going to fall in love with, anyway. It just happens. How about that dashing Nate? He's really a delightful young man. I must admit I find him far more interesting that your friend Rick." Olivia rested her hands on her lap.

Kitty cleared her throat. "I thought I cared enough about Rick to marry him, but now I've changed my mind."

The widow lifted her eyes in a knowing expression. "Life is filled with uncertainties. You can't be sure of anything that a chance act can't change."

"Yes, like having Nate practically tackle me at the door of that awful apartment I was living in." She laughed at the recollection. "I thought he was a mugger."

"Remember, too, that sometimes what we think we want, turns out not to be what we wanted at all."

"But Rick is safe. Nate isn't."

"What do you mean by that—safe?"

"Nate could get . . . killed, like my father."

"Don't dwell on that, Kit, it will only drive you crazy. Remember, most policemen die in their beds of old age."

Kitty changed the subject. "Seaweed's been tossed up all over the place out there on the beach. And plenty of dead fish. Ugh." She purposely didn't tell Olivia about the rotten dinner date with Derek or being rescued by Nate. It was too complicated.

"I'm glad you got home safely last night. Such a storm! I didn't hear you come in."

Kitty shifted in the chair. "It wasn't too late."

She had a strong wish to hand in her resignation after what Andrea's ghastly nephew put her through, but she was determined to hold Andrea to her promise first.

When Kitty came home early from work, she found Olivia sketching on the terrace. She peered over the widow's shoulder and watched in awe.

"Very nice," she said. "I didn't know you were so talented."

Faron, the part-time gardener Olivia had employed for years, was clearing debris from the garden and stacking it near the garage. He was a small, thin man with a battered hat.

"My dear," Olivia said warmly, "I'm so glad you suggested I take up painting again. I'm having such a good time!" She hesitated a moment, then raised the sketch pad. "Do you think this looks anything like a sailboat? It's been so long."

Kitty nodded. Olivia obviously had talent. "Yes, I do. It's really very good. You said you studied art at the Sorbonne."

"Oh yes, dear." Olivia's mouth twitched.

Kitty smiled. Whenever Olivia's mouth twitched, Kitty could be sure what she said was probably a fabrication.

She got up and went to check the mail. Among the assortment of bills and throwaways was a letter from Laurie with a picture. Dressed in baggy beach pajamas and dark sunglasses, she posed glamorously on a low wall, the ocean as a backdrop. Kitty thought her friend looked every inch a movie star.

The short message read: *Are you engaged to Nate yet? Ha! Had a great time. Love, Laurie.*

"You brat!" Kitty muttered.

Then she saw the letter in Nate's handwriting addressed to her and quickly opened the envelope. It was a love letter. She sighed deeply and let a warm smile wash over her face.

True to her word, Andrea Webster placed Kitty's cosmetics on display, and they began to rapidly move off the shelves. Elated, Kitty met Rick for coffee at the hospital cafeteria and gave him a check in the amount she owed him. He wouldn't take any interest. She knew she should break off their relationship then and there, but didn't think it was the proper place. They parted with a light kiss.

In the next few weeks, Kitty quit working for Andrea in order to spend more time with her cosmetics business. Laurie was selling them in California to some of her actress friends. Networking and word of mouth were paying off. Kitty couldn't wait to land a contract with a department store. But that would take time. She had hired a young Cuban-American, Jose Esteban, to help in the small warehouse she had rented. It took grit to quit her job but she was glad now she had taken the leap. Olivia insisted that Kitty rent a tiny shop in the art deco district. Quaking, Kitty took the plunge. The building had blue pillars in front and a wide bay window.

On his day off, Nate came over to install shelves.

"You sure you want me to paint them a pale oyster pink?"

"Yes. What were you thinking?"

"Oh, maybe green."

"Ugh!"

He laughed.

While he worked without a shirt, his sinewy arms glistening, Kitty found it hard to concentrate on her own project.

He stopped a moment and attempted to reach a place between his shoulder blades that had tightened up. She put down the drawer liner paper she was installing and strolled over to massage the troubled spot.

"That's perfect," he said. "Thanks."

"I'm the one who should be thanking you."
He smiled, then returned to painting.

On the shop's grand opening day a busload of tourists arrived. Having a gift of blarney in her soul, Olivia
greeted them as though they were old friends. They
left with sacks full of cosmetics. She added a touch of
class to the small establishment. Kitty had cut Olivia's
hair in the latest fashion and saw to it that her nails
were impeccably done. She was grateful to Olivia,
who wouldn't take a penny for helping out.

"I'll make it up to you someday," Kitty said when
the last customer left for the day and they closed the
door.

Olivia smiled. "You already have, my dear."

"You're a born salesman. You know how to play
on a woman's vanity."

Olivia gave her a coy grin. "Of course. I used to
work at Macy's."

Kitty didn't mention to Olivia at that moment she
was concerned about the fibbing. She'd overheard the
widow making some outrageous claims, like Julia
Roberts shopping there. They'd have to discuss this
very soon and lay down some ground rules.

On Sunday, Kitty slipped into her new bikini and
joined Nate at the Jacuzzi.

"My muscles are so sore," she said, stretching her
arms over her head.

"You wouldn't believe the shop's good week.
Thanks for all your help in making it happen."

He wanted to hear all about it and she spilled out
every detail, except for Olivia's penchant.

"Sounds great. This Jacuzzi'll have us shipshape in

no time," he said, and submerged under the warm water like a seal. Then he came up for air.

His gaze slid over every curve of her body as she got in the water. She hoped he didn't think she was growing fat since she'd put on a couple of pounds over the Christmas holidays. The water swirled around her legs.

She settled herself on a low step. "I hope I haven't bitten off more than I can chew moving in there. I never dreamed I'd open a shop of my own."

His eyes flickered. "With your A-personality you'll do just fine." When he lifted his arm and ran his fingers through his hair, she saw a streak of paint. Enamel was hard to get off. The ginger-colored curly hairs on his arms turned golden in the afternoon sun.

"I hope so," she said, and leaned over to scrape off the paint. He sat close across the short expanse of water. She turned to a table beside the Jacuzzi and poured tea into iced glasses.

When she handed him the drink, he had to fight himself not to draw her into his arms. But he was apprehensive about making a move, even now dreading her rejection, although she had told him she loved him. There was still Rick. Why didn't she break off with him? Having her so near and not being able to touch her was driving him insane. Her long eyelashes fascinated him. Her smile, her cheerful laugh, and the way she lifted her chin, charmed him unbearably.

Strange that she had no understanding of the power she held over him. Although he was usually confident around women, Kitty made him feel different. He knew he must sound like a blithering idiot at times.

Kitty took a sip. Her eyes sparkled over the rim of the glass. "You're awfully quiet, Nate."

He laughed lightly, letting his gaze explore her face. "Just thinking," he said. "Here you are, a real businesswoman. I hope you have all the success in the world. You deserve it."

She threw him a smile. "Thanks for believing in me."

He couldn't help brushing her slim ankle when he adjusted his position. Her flesh felt like silk. She chatted on about what she wanted for the future.

Repositioning himself again, he moved over beside her and rested his arm on the Jacuzzi's lip behind her back. Then he slowly massaged her creamy shoulders. She didn't flinch but murmured a soft, languid sigh, slowly rolling her head from side to side.

"That feels so good. Don't stop," she said.

When he finally pulled his hands away, Kitty sat her glass on the table and gave him an appreciative smile. "Thanks."

She ran her fingernail down the length of his profile. He caught her hand in mid-air and drew it to his lips, kissing the inside of her palm. Unable to resist, he kissed a pink earlobe and caressed the pulse in her throat with his thumb. The act was as natural as breathing. She didn't struggle.

"Darling," he rasped.

Just then a voice called out, "Kit dear, I'm home. Ready to eat?"

They flew apart like teenagers caught necking, and Kitty's face turned scarlet. He'd forgotten Olivia had gone to get fried chicken and potato salad.

"Darn!" he sputtered under his breath, as he heard the French door open wider. Kitty took a deep breath and exhaled.

Chapter Nine

At 11:00 on Monday, Olivia swept into the shop wearing a dated couture suit, her demeanor that of the Queen of Sheba. Kitty had styled her hair, and her long manicured fingernails gleamed a Mandarin red.

"I'm ready to serve the public in my own unique way," she said in a breezy tone.

"You didn't need to come today, Olivia. Remember, we agreed you'd only work a few hours a week. I don't want to tire you."

Olivia smiled, disregarding any arrangement. A customer entered. She turned to the woman in her chatty way. Kitty left the two women and walked back to the tiny back room, bent on taking inventory. She could hear them talking.

Then she stopped dead. Olivia was telling the customer that Luciano Pavarotti had bought cosmetics for his wife from the shop on his last concert tour here.

She sounded as cool as an Hawaiian tradewind. The customer bought a sack full of cosmetics.

After the woman left, Kitty confronted Olivia. "You can't go around tell customers that famous people come in here, let alone buy anything. It's not true."

"But dear, it could be," Olivia reasoned. "If he had known how fine your creams are, I'm quite sure he would have purchased them for Mrs. Pavarotti. Aren't you?"

Kitty had a hard time keeping a straight face in spite of her irritation at Olivia's effrontery, knowing it was probably useless to attempt to change her. The woman was incorrigible, living happily in a world of her own making.

"I can't have you working in here if you tell customers big fibs. Now promise me you won't do it again."

Olivia raised her eyebrows. "Whatever you say, Kit."

Later, Kitty overheard her tell another customer that South Seas had ground pearls in the ingredients, which contained not a mustard seed's worth.

The following day, Kitty dragged herself home after working fourteen hours straight. Olivia took her aside and told her Rick was in the library. The widow discreetly disappeared. An added weight settled on Kitty's weary shoulders. What did he want?

"I wasn't expecting to see you," Kitty said when she came into the library. She took a seat opposite him, not waiting for a friendly kiss.

He fidgeted with his hands. "I haven't been able to

get away since the holidays, so I thought I'd drop by. You look fine."

Kitty picked up on the nervous tic under his eye. *Not enough sleep,* she thought.

"Thanks. It's pretty late." She glanced at her watch. 10:00. "Can I get you a cup of coffee or something?"

"No, that would keep me awake."

"How's your internship going?" She didn't mention that it must be nearly at an end.

"Just great."

"Are they hiring you when it's over?"

"I wish they were, but no, they're not. Actually, I signed on with a hospital in Arizona. Everyone is moving there, I'm told. Great sunshine state, like here."

"But . . ."

He swallowed. "That's what I've been meaning to talk to you about."

"Rick, I could never relocate there." It seemed like a perfect excuse.

He looked almost relieved by her words. "There's something I've been meaning to tell you. I . . ." He cleared his throat loudly, hesitating. A faint upward tug of his lips suggested a wan smile.

She waited for him to go on. Then a thought struck her. "You've found someone else?"

His head went down and his fingers laced together. "Oh, Kitty, I feel like such a heel. Janet and I never meant for it to happen. She's a staff surgical nurse— a splendid woman."

He looked up painfully, forcing himself to meet Kitty's eyes.

"Rick," Kitty said, "you don't need to look like I'm going to shoot you. I don't mind—honestly. Maybe we've just grown apart. I've been putting off saying almost these same words to you for weeks, but couldn't get up the courage."

"I tried," Rick said. Her words hadn't soaked in yet. Then his expression brightened. "You mean it's okay? Oh, my."

"I've been seeing Nate Mansfield. You know, the guy I introduced you to at the ball? At first our relationship was platonic. I honestly wanted to keep it that way. Well, I'm afraid it's gotten out of hand. He's in love with me."

"It's all right. I understand. And you love him?"

"I'm afraid I do."

"You sound almost unhappy. I don't quite understand."

"It's a long story."

They spent the next half hour discussing their new loves.

"Will you marry this man?"

Kitty frowned. "No. He's a policeman, you see."

"I don't see."

"Frankly, I don't want to spend my life worrying about him. I know that sounds selfish, but . . ."

"But don't you worry about him now, married or not?"

Kitty hadn't thought about that. Of course she did, and there was no real way to protect herself from it.

The telephone's incessant rings brought her out of a dead sleep. The warm sun slanted across the bed. Kitty reached over and picked up the receiver, bringing it awkwardly to her ear. "Hello?"

"It's Nate, darling. Sorry I couldn't call last night. I just got off duty."

Kitty spilled out what had happened regarding Rick and his new love.

He laughed wildly. "Great! Just great. Now you don't have to feel guilty." His voice softened to almost a whisper. "I want to marry you, darling, and now you don't have any excuses."

His words, though endearing, didn't solve their dilemma.

"Kitty?"

"I'm here. You took me by surprise."

"And you took me by surprise."

"Nate, I hardly have my eyes open. What a way to greet a girl!"

"When can I see you?"

"I'm busy tonight."

"And I have to work tomorrow night. Darn!"

"Friday evening?"

"I'll pick you up."

"Call me soon."

"You can bet your baby blues on it."

"See you, darling." It was the first time she had called him that and she felt a little shy.

After they disconnected, Kitty jumped out of bed, feeling glorious, and tried to touch the ceiling. She could hardly wait until Friday.

Olivia had suggested Kitty increase the advertising and it was beginning to pay off. Business remained steady. Kitty hired another employee part-time to help with deliveries. His name was Jeff Allenby. Jeff was a young tennis instructor at one of the hotels. He drove around in an old Cadillac convertible, the model with the wings in back. He was tall, sun-bronzed, and good-looking; Olivia called him the Greek Titan. She adored him. When he wasn't working for Kitty or giving tennis lessons, he would sit for Olivia while she painted him in watercolors. He had an easygoing personality and a genuine liking for people. Girls followed him around like puppy dogs. He called them "kittens."

"Don't you admire his fine profile and big muscles, dear?" Olivia asked.

Kitty chuckled, shaking her head. "He doesn't appeal to me. His body might be that of an Adonis, but not his brain." Yet he was easy to have around. She continued to treat him with the same slightly aloof respect as she did Jose, who worked in the warehouse.

Kitty was busier than ever. She was seeing Nate whenever she could squeeze in the time, and their relationship had deepened. She had also perfected a new perfume, Kit's South Sea Pearls.

Olivia told everyone the perfume was "Intoxicating, alluring, and so romantic." Adjectives rolled off her tongue. Kitty believed the perfume would turn out to be her most popular item. Olivia pushed it shamelessly in the shop, buttonholing tourists when she thought Kitty wouldn't catch her.

When Kitty drove home on Saturday night, she slipped a cassette of music into the tapedeck. Listening to the romantic songs made her realize just how much she missed Nate. She hadn't seen him for almost a week.

A siren wailed in the distance. Kitty wondered if he was on a case.

As soon as she arrived home, Olivia insisted on showing her a new dress Yvette had made for her. It was a royal blue color that made her eyes look brighter. With the stock market rising almost daily,

Olivia's poor portfolio was becoming profitable again. She was also planning to have her own art show. Jeff would be the center of many of the paintings.

"If Grandma Moses could do it, so can I," she said. "But you know I'm not that old, Kit."

Kitty swallowed back a chuckle. "I can see tourists going ape over them."

Olivia beamed. The topic of making money always piqued her interest.

"I'll be the first to buy one," Kitty said.

"My dear Kit, you can have any painting you set your heart on."

"Thank you."

Chapter Ten

Nate came by late after work. Olivia had gone to bed. Kitty, although tired, was anxious to see him. He lounged against the fireplace, his well-honed body at ease, his thick lids lowered over his eyes as he watched Kitty with rapt interest.

"I picture you as a prowling puma," she said, grinning, as she put a dish of sandwiches on the coffee table. "Better watch out or Olivia will insist you sit for one of her paintings."

Nate seemed distracted. "So she's going famous on us. Good for her," he said with a half smile.

"Try a sandwich. You look like you could use a snack."

"Maybe later." His gaze angled toward her, a little brooding.

She was instinctively on guard.

"I hate it that we're both so busy," he said, tapping his fingers on the mantle.

131

She saw then how drawn his face looked. "You must have had a taxing week, out there trying to catch the bad guys."

Nate cleared his throat. "Had to be in court all day. What a waste of time. Those lawyers know how to twist things around to make their slimy clients look like altar boys. It really riles me."

"Well, you're not in court now. Want something to drink?"

Nate's posture relaxed a little. "Sure."

"A soft drink okay?"

"Fine."

Nate followed her into the kitchen. She opened a can of cola and started to take a glass down from the cupboard. But he reached for it.

"I forgot you prefer drinking out of the can." She slipped her hands in his pockets while he took a drink.

His eyes brightened. They returned to the library and sat together on the sofa. He ate one of the sandwiches, nodding a thanks.

"Now tell me what else you did today," she said.

"You first." He slipped an arm around her shoulders.

"Cosmetics talk and customers' idiosyncrasies would only bore you."

He took her chin in the palm of his hand and kissed her lips hungrily, "You don't bore me ever, darling."

The following afternoon when Kitty came home, Olivia was abuzz. "Kit, dear, John Hadley, my husband's old business partner, is in town from New York. He's invited us to go to a fund-raising party at Villa Vizcaya next Saturday night. Isn't that wonderful?"

"I don't know. Nate might have the evening off and he'll most likely want to go somewhere."

"Has he mentioned anything?"

"Not yet."

"Well, then, he'll probably have to work. It will be good for your business to be seen hobnobbing with the rich. Oh, I'm so happy."

Olivia's eyes lit up like Roman candles. How could Kitty disappoint her by not going?

"I'll see," she said.

When Kitty called Nate and told him she was going to be tied up, she could hear his disappointment. "So Olivia's old friend invited you?" he said. "How old?"

"Come on, Nate. I'm just going to make her happy." She knew he didn't like it, but why should he be jealous? Hadley was probably old enough to be her father.

"I'll probably have to work, anyway, babe," Nate said. "You and Olivia go on and have a good time."

Kitty had heard about the famous villa but never dreamed of being a guest at the posh mansion. What would she wear? She had seen pictures of guests in the newspapers and knew the rich would dress up for the social event.

"You're awfully quiet tonight, dear," Olivia said when they were seated in front of the TV in the library.

"Don't mind me. I'm just tired."

The doorbell rang and Kitty got up to answer it. Nate stood there, waiting. She threw her arms around his neck and pulled him into a hungry kiss. His possessive arms fastened around her.

"Who is it?" Olivia called.

"It's Nate," Kitty answered, letting her happiness

filter through her voice. She turned her attention back to him and took his hand. "Come on down to my lab. I want to show you something I'm working on."

"Do you mean to do me bodily harm down there in that laboratory?" He mimicked Dr. Frankenstein and she laughed.

He followed her along the hall to the kitchen. She opened the door leading to the cellar and flipped on the light switch. They descended the steps.

"Look, no more clutter," she said, letting her hand flutter around the room.

"Last time I saw this place it was a disaster waiting to happen—stacked boxes, empty crates, and those tiny test tubs you toss around."

"Jose stored everything I don't use often in the warehouse."

Nate took off his navy blue jacket and tossed it on the back of a straight-backed chair. Hands jammed into his trouser pockets, he scouted the room. "Looks neat. Why didn't you let me help?"

"I hesitated to call you since it seems I'm always imposing."

"Imposing? I like to help out. You know I'm at your beck and call."

Nate ran a finger along her throat. The warmth of her silky skin quickly dissolved the lethargic feeling he had experienced earlier.

"I just need to finish up this part of my experiment, as long as I'm down here," she said. "It'll only take a minute or two."

She turned to some project she was working on and he watched her lean over a petri dish on the table, a vial clutched expertly in her fingers. The concentration on her face beguiled him. But then, every move she made stirred him.

"I can just picture you working away down here with the same intensity of Madame Curie." He grinned, enjoying the quick, almost startled way she looked up at him.

Kitty chuckled. She moved across the floor to a little refrigerator, opened it, and took out a jar. "Smell this." She carefully unscrewed the lid and held it under his nose.

"Smells pretty good—not too perfumy."

"You sound like a poor advertising sound-bite! You can be sure I won't use your words—'not too perfumy.' Really! Can't you say something like 'delightful, poignant, out-doorsy?' After all, it's a man's cologne. You're the first to give it the sniff test."

Nate grinned. For a moment his tongue seemed tied in knots while he tried to play the role of an advertising man. "Naw," he said. "I'm not much for flowery speeches. You'll have to get Olivia to help you with that."

"All right, I'll forgive you. By the way, Olivia will be showing her artwork in a gallery in one of the hotels."

"You mentioned it. We'll make sure she has a real turnout. I'll see what I can do down at the station." He resolved right then and there that the widow would have her day or his name wasn't Nate Mansfield.

Kitty screwed the cap back on the jar and returned it to the refrigerator.

Nate found himself scowling. "So you're going to that ritzy party at the villa with all those supercilious types? What did you say the guy's name is? I'll check and see if he has a rap sheet."

She chuckled. "Well, that's a big word! Supercilious. And a rap sheet? You've got to be kidding."

"Don't forget I went to college, too—state college, not Harvard. Besides, you'd be surprised at the number of people with money these days who involve themselves on the dark side in smuggling or money laundering. I—"

Kitty thumped his chest. "Enough! Next thing you'll be telling me he's a gangster. I'm sure Mr. Hadley is a perfect gentlemen."

Nate bristled. "He's probably a stuffed shirt and you'll be bored."

"I'm sorry I mentioned it. Forget I told you."

"Frankly, the idea of your racing off to the Villa Vizcaya so that this guy Hadley can impress you with his rich friends galls me. I know their type. They throw these expensive parties in order to have a good time, and since they call it a charity event, they can write the expenses off on their income taxes. I wonder how much ever actually filters down to the charity."

"You sound bitter."

"Darn right!"

"You don't want me to go, then. Is that it? You're jealous."

Nate saw red. "I'm not jealous! Oh, all right, sure I am."

Kitty shook her head, laughing. "Really, you'd think I was sixteen and didn't know the time of day. It's Olivia's thing. I'm convinced he asked me along just to be nice."

"I'll show you nice!" he said, and reached out for her.

Before she could object, he covered her mouth with a kiss. He opened his eyes long enough to see her eyelids grow heavy-laden while he kissed her throat, her earlobes, the little hollow at the base of her throat.

"I'll make you love me." A hard edge formed around his words. "I'll blot out all the hurt you've ever experienced."

Her sky-blue eyes warmed with emotion. "I think I do love you already."

He released her. "*Think* you do?"

"Yes, I know it."

"You won't be attracted to someone like this rich guy, then?"

"No, I won't. You're being silly."

She straightened her shoulders, annoyed. In an instant he pressed his lips to hers, and in a series of tender kisses she yielded.

He cupped her face in his hands. "No man can love you the way I do."

"Oh, Nate, give me time."

"I'm healthy and young and I love you more than anything. We're both the kind of people who laugh easily, and we're both workaholics. You marry a rich man and he'll expect you to spend your mornings at the Elizabeth Arden salon and your afternoons at the gym working out. And when you turn forty he'll expect you to go on discrete little visits to ye olde plastic surgeon. But I'll still love you even if your face begins to resemble a road map."

Kitty threw her head back and laughed. "You're still thinking about John Hadley. Give me a break, for heaven's sake."

"I need you so much it hurts, darling," he said.

She didn't speak but her lower lip trembled.

"I'm a persistent fool, darling." His voice came out

husky as he appealed to her. "You're my life. Don't you know that?"

She hid her face in his neck. His vision blurred with emotion. Her arms pulled him into a deep kiss, lingering lips against lingering lips.

"I adore you, Kitty, love you with all my heart and soul."

She didn't reply.

"I want to hear you say you love me again."

She swallowed hard. "I do love you, Nate—too much—and it frightens me."

"You have nothing to fear, darling. I'll always love you. Always have, for that matter."

She paused. "I don't know . . ."

"Tell me what's troubling you."

His heart was full, as he thought of marriage.

"Because . . ." Her voice trailed off.

Then it hit him and he understood. Her father. That awful trauma. She couldn't seem to set it aside.

"I won't leave you, darling. I'll always be here for you—promise."

"Don't make a promise you have no control over," she said with a catch in her throat, "with the work you're involved in."

He tightened his arms protectively around her and tried to soothe her.

When Kitty arrived home from work the next day a fragrant bouquet of snow-white peonies was waiting for her. The card read. *These foolish things remind me of you. Love, Nate.* She thought about the words, which came from a romantic old song, one of her favorites. She broke into a smile, wondering how in the world he found peonies at this time of year.

Chapter Eleven

When John Hadley came for Olivia and Kitty in a Rolls-Royce to take them to the party at Villa Vizcaya, he hardly took his eyes off Kitty. It made her uncomfortable. She wore a white silk dress expertly made over by Yvette, Olivia's dressmaker. It hung in a becoming cowl effect, draping the front, with wide crisscross straps in the back. The contrast between the dress and her coppery hair was stunning, Olivia had told her.

When they arrived the window glowed with joy. "These people are dressed to the nines," she whispered in Kitty's ear. "I've been rich and I've been poor, and rich is better!" She glanced down at her once-aging gown and her eyes twinkled. In the sweeping style she preferred, the made-over garment could have come straight from a Fifth Avenue fashion salon.

Two acquaintances who arrived at about the same

139

time, came over to greet her. They were dressed in chic black.

"Dear Olivia, you look positively divine!" the older woman gushed. "You must have a new hairdresser. Very chic! Tell us who."

Olivia smiled coyly, her lips twitching. "Not on your life, Bettina. My girl only has time for me."

Kitty fanned her hand across her mouth, hiding a grin, while Olivia breezed regally by them.

Nestled in an exotic setting of pools and Italian gardens, fountains and statues, the Italian Renaissance–style villa had once been the showplace of South Florida and was now a museum. Rare European antiques and Rococo and Neoclassical furnishings gave Kitty the feeling she must be in a castle on the Riviera. The high carved ceiling and Italian marble added to the home's rich ambiance.

In the crush of people, Hadley found the table he'd reserved. Two couples were already there, and he introduced Kitty. Olivia knew them.

"These are my old friends and associates from new York, Kit," Hadley said. "Harry and Louisa Thornton and Ralph and Joan Ryder."

They said their hellos.

"We always come to Florida for at least two months every year," Louisa Thornton said. "New York is so ghastly in the winter."

Kitty wondered why, if they came that often, they never stopped by to see Olivia. Maybe she wasn't rich enough anymore. The haughty, dark-eyed woman, extremely thin, gazed at Kitty without a smile. Her gray silk gown was of the finest material, and the diamond-and-star-sapphire brooch on her dress was exquisite.

Joan Ryder also scanned Kitty, making her feel like a bug under a researcher's glass.

"You must join us for cocktails soon, John," Louisa said. She and Joan leaned close to him and talked in confidential tones. Olivia bent forward to listen, while Kitty hung back.

"Are you bidding on a painting tonight, John?" Joan asked. "I saw one I particularly like. It is really quite good. I could swear that man standing over there posed for it." She pointed her long, manicured finger, then pouted. "Ah, he's out of sight now. Such gorgeous ginger-colored hair, and what broad shoulders. I thought perhaps he might agree to a sitting—say on one of my horses."

"You could call your painting 'The Country Squire'," Louisa said.

"Yes. I have the perfect place for it in our country home in Virginia."

Kitty's stomach turned over. Had Nate come after all? She never knew when he was going to show up. She searched through the crowd, but couldn't catch a glimpse of him anywhere. Disappointed, she turned back to the gathering around the table, wishing she had stayed home. These people seemed out of her league.

Hadley turned to Kitty. "Joan's a horsewoman and has lots of trophies and ribbons to prove it. Goes fox hunting in England."

"I admit I love the chase." Joan's voice livened. "There's something wonderful about being on the back of a spirited animal riding to hounds."

Her husband adjusted his thick glasses. He seemed to have lost interest. "She's got a few broken bones for her efforts, too," he added with a shrug.

Harry Thornton gave a wry smile, apparently enjoying the frown that creased Joan Ryder's face. He took out a cigarette and a gold lighter and lit up. "Can't abide horses, myself," he said. "And those pretentious fox hunts! Puts me in mind of people trying to emulate the English gentry. I'd much rather hunt big game in Africa. Now there's an adversary!"

Kitty gritted her teeth. Before she thought, she spoke her thoughts out loud. "I equate hunting unarmed animals with shooting ducks in a barrel, and just about as fair."

All eyes glittered on her. Hadley roared with laughter, as did the other men, but the wives looked disapproving. Olivia grinned. Embarrassed by her own rash comment, Kitty knew she'd probably made enemies.

Hadley pushed back his chair. "Shall we circulate, Kit?"

Relieved, she didn't hesitate. "Let's."

Hadley ushered her through the crowd. He wore a white dinner jacket that added to his distinguished appearance, his hair neatly cut, the gray showing at the temples.

He raised his hand, acknowledging several acquaintances. "I think everyone in town is here," he said.

Kitty glanced around, feeling out of her element, although she recognized a few familiar faces—mostly Olivia's friends and some old clients. Hadley shouldered his way to the bar.

When he came back, he handed her a long-stemmed glass. "You look beautiful tonight."

Just as she was about to thank him, a short, balding man with a pot belly bumped into Hadley and turned to apologize profusely.

"Why, if it isn't John Hadley, my old lawyer!" A long-legged, blond showgirl–type batted her heavy mascara-thick eyes over his shoulder. "Good to see you, old friend." He pumped Hadley's hand, giving Kitty an appreciative once-over.

Hadley appeared to be trying to remember the man's name, his mouth working.

"You haven't forgotten me? Milos Brotherton Horning! You saved my scalp on that nasty business a couple of years ago." His myopic gaze swung back to Kitty. "Your daddy here, kept the big boys from taking over my manufacturing business. They knew very well it would take me a little time to pay off the notes. But I'm riding high now, I'll tell you."

Kitty felt more than saw Hadley flinch, and wondered why he didn't introduce them.

"Ah, yes," Hadley said with little enthusiasm. "Nice to see you again. I hope things continue to work out." He nodded, his shoulders stiff, and took Kitty by the arm, turning away.

The man snickered and called out, "Let's get together for a few drinks later on. Our girls probably have a lot in common. Hee hee!"

Hadley didn't look back or acknowledge the invitation. Perhaps he resented the reference to being called "daddy," Kitty thought. Or had the man meant sugar-daddy? She grimaced.

Hadley possessed a commanding voice. "It's warm in here. Let's get a shot of fresh air. I want to show you the bay in moonlight."

"Yes, it is warm tonight."

He took Kitty's hand and navigated among the throng of people until they stepped out on the verandah. She followed him down a flight of steps leading to an unusual sculptured barge at the edge of the water. A full moon cast golden shimmers on the sea, and the North Star sparkled like a beacon through the rhinestone-studded sky.

"Can you tell me what Vizcaya means?" Kitty asked. She felt more like herself away from his friends.

Hadley thought a moment and set his glass on a railing. "I think someone told me it means 'elevated place.' "

"The name sounds far more mysterious than what it actually means, then," she said.

He move closer. Kitty felt his breath on her face and took a step back. The man was coming on to her. Where was Olivia when she needed her?

"It's wonderful to see Olivia looking so well," he said, as though reading her mind. "Hubert's death had to be awfully tough on her. A gem of a fellow! When I first went to work for the firm I now head, he was a senior partner. Hubert taught me a lot." He paused. "I didn't know Olivia had a niece as lovely as you."

Kitty barely caught the smile on his mouth in the moonlight, but she responded with candor. "I'm not really her niece. Just a good friend. If you know Olivia well, you'll understand she sometimes likes to exaggerate."

He didn't speak for a moment, the lawyer in him probably analyzing their connection, given the difference in their ages. But he let it go and amused himself by telling her a little about his life and humble beginnings in Kansas City.

"I can afford caviar but prefer a good Kansas City steak," he said. "I guess you could say I'm a simple-enough guy."

"You're life sounds interesting." Kitty set her own empty glass next to his.

He leaned back on his heels. "I wouldn't be honest if I didn't admit I appreciate the good things that prosperity can bring to a man." His eyes traveled over her. "Kit, I like you. You don't fawn, and you're a little standoffish. My instincts tell me you're the kind of woman I want to get to know better. Olivia tells me you're in business. Commendable. Perhaps I can help you in some way. Possibly some backing for a new venture?" He took a moment, lifted her hand, and raised it to his lips.

Kitty pulled her hand away. Her breath caught in her throat, and she didn't know what to say. His not-so-subtle words and actions weren't what she had expected of so distinguished a man. Now she understood Nate's apparent concern. She had thought he was just being funny.

"I'm flattered, John, but I really don't need any help. And," she added, "I already have a relationship. Do you mind if we go back inside now? Olivia is probably wondering what happened to us."

Without waiting for John's reply, she started toward the steps leading to the house above.

He caught up to her. "I didn't mean to monopolize you." His voice sounded almost cold.

"It's a lovely night," she said, changing the subject as she began the climb.

"I have to say you remind me of a painting of Aphrodite in the moonlight out here."

"Thanks." He tried to grab her hand but she resisted. *This man really has a line,* she thought.

They joined the others at the table. Olivia smiled as Kitty took the eat next to her.

"I'm having an outstanding time! Just everybody's here," Olivia said in her airy fashion. "How about you two?" She winked at them. "Enjoying yourselves, my dears?"

"Oh, very much," Kitty lied, wondering if she dared complain of a headache and take a taxi home. Here she was, surrounded by people, and all she could think about was Nate.

Chapter Twelve

When Kitty went to work the next day the sky had been a brilliant blue. Now, while she sat in a coffee shop, munching a boiled ham sandwich on her lunch break, she noticed it had turned to the color of mushroom soup outside. Another storm was moving in. The atmosphere of gloom mirrored her mood. Several days had passed since she heard from Nate. Maybe he was punishing her, but he didn't seem the type.

John Hadley had sent sprays of pink orchids after the party to both her and Olivia. He left a message on her answering machine, saying he would be back in town in a week and wanted to see her again. The man didn't give up easily. He might be agreeable and charming but he could forget about her having any interest in him. She had only agreed to go to the villa to please Olivia.

All at once a clap of thunder startled her, followed by another. Sometimes the universe seemed in chaos, she thought. Did everything happen by chance or was there some great scheme in all this?

Kitty took a sip of coffee. There never seemed to be enough time. She was always in a rush. She'd bolted half her sandwich down and it felt like a dead weight sitting in her stomach.

A college-age waiter came and refilled her cup. It was a cozy place to eat. She looked up to see Nate striding toward her, and the sounds around her instantly died away.

When Nate came in and saw Kitty alone at a table near the entrance, he stood there watching her for a few moments, and let a smile light up his face. Just as he started to take a step, a clap of thunder jarred the floor under his shoes. She jumped and looked out the window. The middle-aged owner behind the counter laughed, then went back to joking with a patron.

Nate was glad to see the welcoming smile on Kitty's face. "Hi." He pulled out a chair and sat down.

"I wish you had come earlier," she said. "I was just finishing. But I'll stay for a little while if you're going to order something. Maybe you want the other half of my sandwich."

Thunder crackled again, and he could feel the hairs on his arms rise with the electricity.

"I only have time for coffee." The waiter came over and Nate ordered.

He reached across the table to take one of her leftover French fries and popped it in his mouth. It was cold. "I've missed you," he said.

"Me, too."

They made small talk as he finally ate the sandwich on her plate. But he didn't ask if she had a good time at the villa. He was still miffed that she went, not asking himself why he was jealous of a man probably old enough to be her father. However, he knew some of these old guys preferred young women on their arms, and had the money to attract a pretty face.

Kitty glanced at her wristwatch. "Do you know we've been talking nearly a half-hour? Olivia's filling in for me and I promised I wouldn't be long. She's got a bridge game this afternoon." She snapped up the bill and opened her purse to take out her wallet.

"No," he said, "I'll get it."

He crammed his hand in his pocket, drew out enough money to cover the check and a tip, and tossed it on the table.

"You don't need to do that," she said.

He didn't reply to her protestations. "I'll drive you back. We can talk in the Jeep."

"Thanks for the lunch."

He tossed her a grin and took her elbow. By the time they reached the parking garage it had started to sprinkle. He opened the door for her, glad he had left the top on.

He slid in beside her. "Want to go to the department's annual picnic this Sunday? It's being held at the surfing beach where I took you a while back."

"Sounds like fun. Count me in."

Happy, Nate felt a grin broaden across his face. He drove her to the front door of the shop. She got out, giving him a lovely smile and a little wave of the hand. He watched her go inside. Even her walk was cute. Then he hit the steering wheel and whistled. She was too adorable for words.

* * *

When Nate picked up Kitty, he looked tired and shadows marked the planes of his face. She thought about the dangers that lurked in his workaday world—so different from hers. He was a mystery, dealing with heaven only knew what kind of people, yet he never complained about his work. That part of him was a stranger to her and he guarded it scrupulously. She remembered him saying once when they were kids that he was going into police work because he wanted to make the world a safer place. But she was still having a hard time adjusting to it.

They reached the beach and headed for a spot on the sand. Kitty hadn't met most of the officers, department personnel, and their families. Eric came up and helped spread the blanket. Nate went back to the car to get the beach umbrella. She sat down to watch the boys and girls play in the surf.

A couple, Tony and Amanda Ryan, came by and introduced themselves, then another couple joined them—the Williamses. Kitty liked them.

When they left, Eric said, "I'll go get us something to drink."

"Make mine a Coke," she said. "And thanks."

Nate set up the umbrella and eased down beside her, pulling off his shirt, exposing his tanned chest.

"Go on and take a swim," Kitty said. "Eric's gone to get us something cold to drink." She looked around at the white sand, blue-green sea, and a bright sky with a few billowing clouds far out on the horizon. "Gosh, it's beautiful out here. So peaceful."

"It's paradise."

Near the water's edge she saw the man Nate introduced her to when she still lived in that awful apartment. *Jack,* she thought—that was his name. He took off his sunglasses and stared at her, smiling. She smiled back. His chest glistened with tanning oil. He put on his sunglasses and strolled away.

Nate spoke up. "How about a swim?"

"Brr. I remember how cold the water can be this time of year. I think I'll beg off."

"I'm sure I won't be in long, either. When I get back we'll round up some of the gang for a volleyball game. Okay?"

"Great." He looked so boyishly excited that she acted enthusiastic, even though she hadn't played volleyball since high school. She watched him run toward the water, admiring his strong, masculine grace. Eric came back, handed her an open Coke, and slouched down on the blanket, following her gaze.

"That guy's crazy about you, Kitty."

"You exaggerate." She didn't want to discuss something so personal with Eric.

"Naw, I'm dead right." He laughed playfully and leaned back on his elbows. "Let me tell you a little something about love. For me it runs in cycles—comes and goes. But it's not like that with Nate. All he can talk about is you this and you that."

"Eric, really."

He gave her a lopsided smile. "See that gal over there in the skimpy bikini, the one with the mile-long legs? She's been trying to nab 'ol Nate for a long time."

Kitty looked a little closer. Sure enough, a very attractive woman had her arm through his. Why wasn't he in the water swimming? That's where he had been heading.

"Her name's Lynne Matson—a dispatcher with the

department downtown. And boy, does she have a thing for him."

"Interesting," Kitty said. She couldn't take her eyes off the woman. Lynne's hair was jet black and she had a to-die-for tan. Kitty lifted the soft drink to her lips just as the woman lifted a can to hers, revealing a swanlike neck. Lynne offered the can to Nate, a coy gleam in her dark eyes. He declined. Kitty wondered if there had been something between them—and the green-eyed monster crept over her. Then he dashed off for the water.

Eric gave her an odd look, as though waiting for her to comment.

"Nate's never mentioned her," Kitty said, keeping her voice indifferent. She drew her gaze away from the woman and examined a chipped fingernail. Eric seemed to lose interest. She turned her attention to the others on the beach. They seemed to be having more fun than the guests at the posh villa party. Some of the children flew colorful kites shaped like bats, fish, and octopuses, while others built sand castles.

Nate came back and Eric left to get a hot dog, giving her a knowing flick of the eye over his shoulder. Nate's body dripped saltwater, his stomach muscles as hard as a washboard. She stared briefly, admiring him. He picked up a towel to dry himself off.

"You're right," he said. "The water's too cold for anything but jellyfish."

Kitty laughed. "You liked it, anyway."

He nodded and tossed the towel on the sand. She took out a bottle of sunblock from her beach bag and slathered her shapely legs. He lounged beside her on the blanket, watching her languid movements.

On impulse, he reached out to reposition a lock of

her coppery hair that blew across her face in the sea breeze. The texture of it between his fingers reminded him of satin. Kitty filled him with wonder—so different from pushy Lynne Matson. Kitty glanced up, her moist lips slightly parted, a look he could die for, and his blood heated.

For a moment he forgot they were at the beach surrounded by his working buddies. *Get a grip,* he chastised himself, lying down on his side and closing his eyes. This was no time for amorous thoughts.

"You love the beach, don't you?" she said.

"I love you more." She chuckled. He cleared his throat. "Yeah. It's a great place."

Sometimes he liked to escape the grim, seedy parts of town that were his beat, and come here alone to surf. It was a place where a sunny sky caressed the sandy beach. Somehow, he came alive with the smell of the ocean. It was as close to Eden as he figured he'd ever get.

Nate pulled himself into a sitting position and glanced around. "Time for that volleyball game." He jumped up.

Kitty hesitated, not so sure she wanted to participate in the game now that Lynne Matson would probably be playing. Nate ran on ahead, gathering up players. Kitty watched his smooth pectoral muscles flex, admiring the fast way he moved. Reluctantly, she followed him to the volleyball net. Others were already assembling.

Nate pointed to Kitty. "You're on my team, babe."

She nodded, grateful.

They chose up sides, with Lynne Matson across the net. The better to be observed, Kitty thought, trying to keep her face from looking spiteful. The woman had a gorgeous figure and she seemed to know all the right moves to display it.

Before Kitty realized what was happening, Lynne fired the ball directly at her. The force of it nearly knocked her off her feet, but she managed somehow to get it back across the net. Lynne snickered. Another team member pounded it back.

Eric, next to Kitty, let go a hearty laugh. "Hey, Lynne, I hear you're quitting your job so you can join a national women's volleyball pro-team. That right?"

He ducked as she aimed one square at his head. "Not likely, you idiot," she spat.

Lynne apparently enjoyed showing off her athletic prowess. Kitty tried to hide her lack of sportsmanly talent or her jealous irritation.

When it was Kitty's turn to serve, Lynne stood with her hands on her sleek hips, legs wide apart, an icy glimmer in her eyes. The ball made a weak arc over the net. Kitty was so humiliated she wanted to slink away but knew she couldn't give up. Nate and Eric rooted for her.

She wrinkled her nose. *You're not the only gutsy gal around here,* she silently hissed at the woman on the other side of the net. By the time they switched sides she was getting the hang of it, diving for low balls with the best of them.

Jack stood on the sidelines, grinning. When Kitty served a fast ball across the net, he clapped. "Cool," he said.

Kitty turned and waved.

When it was over, Nate hugged her. "You were super!"

Lynne slunk away with another man. Nate could see

Kitty felt pretty good. She grinned most becomingly as they started back to their place on the beach.

Along the way, he picked up a sandy-haired little boy. Jimmy Ryan was the son of Nate's friends whom Kitty had met earlier. Nate placed him on his shoulders. Jimmy let out a giggle. Nate took off galloping along the surf like a horse, holding the boy's feet securely. The child squealed with delight. Kitty followed. They ran in and out of the water, the bubbling foam creeping up their ankles.

When they came back, Nate returned Jimmy to his parents, although the boy wanted another ride. Kitty sat down and scuffed her feet in the moist sand. He placed his hand on her back.

"Bored?"

She looked up at him and smiled. "No way. But you've worn me out."

He felt a deep joy. "What a great day this is."

"And I was just thinking how wonderful you are," she said.

He grinned, surprised by her endearing words. "So you finally figured that out?"

"You're also brash. Lie down here beside me, Nate." She patted the blanket and leaned back.

He laid down as she directed and she ran a finger over his chin. Then he propped himself and kissed her.

She glanced around, then back to him. "We're not alone, remember?"

He groaned. "To my everlasting disappointment."

She chuckled.

After a while, the beach party broke up and people went their separate ways.

Before sundown, they changed clothes and Nate

drove Kitty to Joe's Corral for dinner. It had been one of the best days of his life.

The following Saturday, a splendid morning after an early squall, Nate took Kitty sailing. It was the day of Olivia's exhibit. Kitty felt an exhilaration she had never experienced. The twenty-five-foot sailboat he had borrowed skimmed the turquoise-blue water, spewing cool foam in her face. The air was fresh and clear, and the salty sea-breeze teased her hair.

Nate tacked in the wind, letting the sails billow. She knew he was a man accustomed to being in control, and he performed his sailor duties with little effort. In the distance innocuous stratus clouds formed, adding to the picture-perfect scene.

Kitty wished she had worn slacks instead of shorts and a tank top. Out on the water, the weather was cooler than she had expected. Nate wore only cutoffs, seemingly unaffected, his strong legs rolling with the waves. The sun shone on his tanned body, turning the hairs on his arms and chest to curling gold. He set the sails, came over to where she reclined, and took her in his steel-like arms.

"We're finally totally and utterly alone. Frightened?"

He gave her an unexpectedly intense kiss that thrilled her. When she came up for air, he merely grinned and moved aft to turn on the radio.

"What was that all about?" she asked when he came back.

He laughed. "That was for all the times I wanted to and didn't."

"I could get used to this—sailing along like Cleopatra on the Nile," she said, stretching.

Then a dark mood invaded her thoughts. Nate was decent and unpretentious, and Kitty admired him as much as she loved him. But could she ever marry someone on the force? A maze of doubts plagued her, yet she made up her mind to push them away. No sense in spoiling their morning.

They sailed around the bay for over an hour. Nate was like a kid with a new toy. Being out on the water with him relaxed her more than anything had in a long while.

By the time Kitty got home, Olivia was as nervous as a cat showing off her kittens for the first time. She insisted on getting to the gallery hours early, even though the showing wouldn't begin until 8:00. Then she changed her mind. When it was nearly time to leave, Olivia disappeared altogether. Kitty was miffed that she would go off without telling her.

Nate came by and Kitty left with him, telling him of her concern for Olivia's whereabouts. "Excited or not, she should have told me she was leaving!"

"This is a big deal for her," Nate said. "Maybe she got stage fright."

"Oh, wouldn't that be just awful if she decided not to show up at all?"

"She'll be there, believe me."

"I won't relax until this thing is over."

He grinned. "Stop worrying. You look beautiful in your blue dress. That shade matches your eyes."

"Stop trying to butter me up. I want to stay in a dither."

He laughed, and drove on to the hotel.

Olivia emerged fashionably late at the gallery, making a grand entrance on the arm of Jeff Allenby, her model. He wore a rented white tuxedo. She smiled graciously like a queen to her adoring subjects. Kitty had done Olivia's hair and nails earlier, but her makeup was a bit heavy-handed.

Olivia strolled over to Kitty and Nate and kissed their cheeks.

"Darlings, I'm so glad you could make it."

"You look super," Nate said. He nodded to Jeff.

Olivia fluttered her hand nervously. Kitty wanted to say, "Olivia, where the devil have you been?" But she merely smiled. This was Olivia's big night. Then Olivia hurried away, still on Jeff's arm, to greet one of the couples John Hadley had introduced Kitty to at the Villa Vizcaya.

Kitty recognized some of the people who had been at the policeman's beach picnic and others who attended the villa affair. They stood with glasses in hand, viewing Olivia's work with favorable remarks. She wondered if both Nate and John had twisted some arms.

"I'm overwhelmed," Kitty said. "I had no idea there'd be such a turnout."

"I told a few friends about it." Nate casually straightened his tie. "Looks like they took my suggestion."

"I would say so!" She cast him a questioning stare. "Did you threaten to arrest them if they didn't show up?"

He grinned but didn't reply. She flew away to greet someone else.

"I hope my mom and Uncle Joe get here in time," Kitty said. She fidgeted with a button.

Olivia came back, her face as animated as a bride's. She wore a new violet diaphanous gown with peacock feathers on the shoulder, one of Yvette's finest creations.

"You wouldn't believe it. I just talked to an art critic from the Miami paper. And he told me my work is fabulous! Well, he didn't use that word exactly, but I got the gist of it all the same."

"I'm happy for you," Kitty said. "The critic's right, your paintings are lovely."

Someone called her name and Olivia flitted off again. Nate was about to take Kitty's hand and move on, when John Hadley joined them. Nate involuntarily stiffened, thinking this must be the man Kitty had described.

"How nice to see you, Kit," Hadley said. He ignored Nate, his eyes traveling over her.

"Nice to see you, too," she said. "This is my friend, Nate Mansfield. Nate, John Hadley."

Nate inclined his head as they exchanged a polite handshake. He instinctively didn't like Hadley. The man looked too self-assured, typical of so many lawyers.

"I'm going to buy one of Olivia's paintings for my New York office, Kit. Will you pick it out for me? It'll remind me of you and Olivia basking here in the sun while I'm enduring another gruesome winter." John's eyes glittered.

"Sure." She pointed to one on the wall to her right. "This one's lovely. Sails unfurling. How about it?"

He coughed. "Oh, yes, it is nice. But I was thinking we might browse among them first."

Kitty smiled. "I wish I could, but I'm afraid I don't have time."

He looked disappointed, but thanked her in his courteous manner, nodded to Nate, and moved on.

Mary and Joe found Kitty and Nate, and traded hugs.

"Olivia will be happy you made it," Kitty said.

Mary wore a navy blue suit, the jacket a shade too tight. She turned to Joe. "Come on. I want first pick at one of these paintings. Olivia's going to become famous, I just know it. We'll see you two later on."

Nate took Kitty's hand. "Let's find a corner away from this crowd."

They threaded through the people. Eric caught up to them and tapped Nate on the shoulder. "I don't know anything about art, Nate. I'm a bachelor. What do I want with an original painting hanging in my bathroom? I only came because you insisted. Now show me something not too expensive I can buy, so I can get the heck out of here."

Nate glowered. "Hang it in the living room, for heaven's sake. Or give it to your mother for her birthday, for all I care. Just buy one. It's important." He glanced at Kitty, wishing they could get out of here, too. It wasn't his kind of thing.

Nate had been equally demanding to some of his other friends, and he felt a twinge of guilt. But Olivia's success was important to him. He liked people who accomplished things. And he'd already bought two.

"Okay. If you say so," Eric said.

Nate slapped him on the back. "Good buddy!"

Eric wandered off. Moving through the crowd, Nate heard people making comments. "Mrs. Christenson has a Cézanne sensitivity." And, "She makes excellent use of shading and accents." Another said, "Such lively elements." And he smiled to himself. They probably didn't know any more about art than he did.

Olivia had a circle of people around her when he

saw her again. "Art transcends the passage of time," she told them. They all nodded knowingly. "And . . ."

Yeah, she must have kissed the Blarney Stone somewhere along the way in her life. He grinned.

Kitty had gone to check on sales. Nate stood off to himself, hands thrust in pockets, observing the goings-on and counting heads. The art dealer couldn't have asked for a better turnout.

Kitty came back and handed him a long-stemmed glass, her face animated. He took a sip. Just seeing her that way made him happy.

"This is going unbelievably well," she said.

"I'm glad. Nice gathering."

"I'll bet you buttonholed half the people here."

"Not me," he said with a straight face.

She slipped her arm through his. "Let's step outside and get a breath of fresh air."

"You were reading my mind."

Chapter Thirteen

When Kitty backed the car into the street the next morning, she could still remember the incredible power of Nate's good-night kiss. It sent a little thrill through her. Thoughts of the art exhibit's success made her feel good, too. John Hadley had cornered her later before the show ended and pressed her to go out with him. She had politely turned aside his request. She wasn't about to get involved with two men again.

At the warehouse lab, she analyzed a new sample. Her concentration was so intense that she almost didn't hear the delivery man come in. He carried two dozen long-stemmed red roses and a broad smile.

"Oh, my! For me?"

"If your name's Kitty O'Hara." He glanced around.

"That's me." He sat the bouquet on the counter and she signed for it, giving him a tip.

The tiny florist's envelope was almost lost in the velvety flowers, but she picked it out and read the

162

card: *You're never far from my thoughts. Love you, darling. Nate.*

Feeling flattered, she grinned. A sudden longing swept over her. Why couldn't she let go completely— commit to him? Why did she torment herself with doubts? She bit her lip, wondering how long he would be patient. There were surely more Lynne Matsons and Laurie Kingstons around just waiting in the wings.

That night, bone-tired, Kitty slipped between the cool sheets. She lay on her back, gazed up at the dark ceiling, and thought about Nate and the lovely flowers. No man had ever stirred the fire in her soul quite like he managed to do. She almost got up to look down the street, just to see if his Jeep might be parked out there. He could turn up at the oddest times. The thought made her feel warm inside, and she dropped off to sleep.

In the wee hours of the morning, Kitty awoke with a start, one leg tingling. It went from tingling to feeling like a wet, lifeless sponge. She jumped up and hopped around the dark room until the feeling returned. Outside the open French doors, the moon resembled a giant pearl. It cast silvery shadows over the rug. She lay back down. Painful images that had started as a dream emerged with clarity, dark and frightening. Something rooted in her childhood? Of course—her father's death. She laid back down. Would the shock of his untimely death always torment her?

Nate clamped the telephone receiver to his ear. He had called several times before Kitty finally answered.

She didn't sound like herself. He said he'd come by when he got off duty.

Kitty met him at the door and they went back to the library. Olivia was away playing bridge.

He brushed a kiss across her cheek. "You look tired. Didn't sleep well last night?"

She nodded, and took a seat, leaning back against the cushion. "I guess I'm really mixed up. I keep having these nightmares about my dad."

"I'm sorry, darling. It must have been awful for you."

Kitty looked into his concerned eyes and absorbed their comfort. "But why do I have them after all these years?"

"Maybe it's because you haven't come to grips with it. You're afraid it might happen to someone else you care for."

"I never thought of that."

"No matter how much a person wants to, hanging on too tight won't make a difference when the time comes. You've just got to live in the here and now."

"It's hard."

He pulled her out of the chair and put his hands on her shoulders. "You don't have to go it alone." He kissed her cheek. "Let's go get something to eat. I'll bet you haven't had a solid meal today."

"I'll need to go change first. I look a sight." Kitty glanced down at her wrinkled jeans.

"Why? We're only going to my place," he said.

"Oh! Okay. I've never been there."

Nate drove out of the city and turned off on a rural road. His house was tucked away along a peaceful residential street of palmettos and tropical foliage. A big dog came bounding up, tail wagging, friendly eyes excited. It was the largest dog she had ever seen.

"Awesome!" Nate said. The dog jumped up and gave his face a slurp.

Kitty admired him, tentatively holding out her hand.

"That's his name—Awesome," he told her.

She found herself smiling. "He's as big as a horse. Where's his saddle?"

Nate grinned. "He's a greyhound. Got him from one of those rescue places. And no, I don't saddle him up."

The dog raced on ahead to the house and disappeared. Kitty followed Nate.

Vines covered nearly everything. "I think I'm in the jungle," she said.

"You are. There's a swamp not far from here."

Nate opened the door and Kitty realized it hadn't been locked.

"Lose your key?" she asked.

"Don't need one with Awesome around."

A cool breeze wafted through the large open windows. The rustic interior had three large rooms that opened into one another—a living room, kitchen and bedroom.

"I designed this place myself and built a good portion of it," Nate said with a touch of pride. "This open design helps to keep the house cool by allowing the heat to escape. Got the idea after vacationing in the Caribbean."

"It looks comfortably masculine," she said. "And the wooden floors are nice."

Nate watched her take in everything. "Not like my tree house back home, huh?"

Kitty chuckled. "A far cry."

"Take a seat and I'll get you something to drink. What'll it be?"

"A glass of mineral water would be fine, if you have it." She took a seat on a leather couch and brought her legs up under her. He thought she looked wan.

Awesome stood watching, his large eyes unfathomable. Kitty called his name and he obediently came over and sat by her. She reached down to stroke his short tan coat.

Nate brought back a glass and handed it to her. Then he bent and kissed her neck where her shoulder met. She took a sip, letting its coolness tingle in her throat. He had added a slice of lemon.

"I'll put on some music," Nate said. He thumbed through a stack of CDs in a box in the corner and withdrew one. "You'll like this. Soft and mellow." He inserted it in a player. The music came on.

"Nice," she said.

He slouched into a large, low-slung West Indies chair, extended his long legs, and kicked off his shoes. "Might as well get comfortable."

Kitty slipped out of her sandals and placed them opposite the dog. She turned to look at his makeshift bookcase. His choice of books ranged from old copies of Louis L'Amour westerns, to John le Carre's spy mysteries and classics like Charles Dickens and Rudyard Kipling. There didn't seem to be any current authors.

"I like to read when I have time," he said.

"You always did." She shifted on the couch.

He picked up a picture from an end table and dusted it off with his shirt tail before handing it over to her. "It's you."

She examined the old photo and smiled. "Me? I was never that skinny."

"You sure filled out real nice." He moved his hands in waves, grinning.

She gave him a mock shove. "I wonder how old I was."

"Your fourteenth birthday. I wrote it on the back."

She grimaced. "Look at the braces."

"Braces? I never noticed."

"Liar."

He hefted himself up. "I'm going to barbecue the steaks now. Still like yours medium rare?"

"Sure. But isn't it awfully late to be barbecuing? Maybe you could open up a can of soup."

"Nothing's too good for you, kid."

"Then let me help."

"You can fix the salad. I'm not big on that."

He unslung his legs and got to his feet. "Hope you find everything you need. I don't exactly have a gourmet kitchen."

She followed him to the kitchen. Awesome thumped along at Nate's heels. Nate took steaks out of the refrigerator, laid them on the counter, and rubbed the meat with garlic and onions. The tantalizing aroma made Kitty's stomach churn with hunger. It was the first time she'd felt hungry today.

Nate was right. His kitchen was tidy but not well equipped. She took the salad fixings from the refrigerator and placed them in the sink, washing them off. He slid back a glass door and went out to the patio to light the barbecue. She searched for a vegetable paring knife, gave up, and used a steak knife instead. The simple act of preparing a salad helped bring her back to reality.

Nate came in, fed the dog from a large sack of dry food, then disappeared again. In a little while, he brought the steaks back on a sizzling platter. Kitty had the salad ready.

They sat down side-by-side. She ate ravenously, as though it were her first meal in a week.

"This is wonderful," she said between bites. "Somehow it seems strange sitting here at your kitchen table, eating steak fashionably late."

Nate grinned. "Glad you like it."

A contentment settled over her. "I'm eating like a pig."

"I know."

She laughed. "You could say it wasn't true."

He only shrugged.

Afterward, they washed the dishes together.

"Let's kick back now," he said when they finished.

"You've developed quite a talent for barbecuing," Kitty said over her shoulder when she hung the dish cloth on the refrigerator handle.

"Yeah, I am pretty good." He laughed at his own bragging.

She followed him back into the living room. "Thanks for everything, Nate."

"You don't need to say that." His voice was softly endearing.

She took the couch and he sat down on the floor beside her, his arm draped over her knees. "Sorry, I don't have any dessert," he said.

She held her full stomach, and exaggerated its size with her hands. "I don't know where I'd put it."

Nate glanced across the room to where it connected with the bedroom, then glanced back to her. He rose and sat down beside her. With a tender gesture, he cupped her face in his palms and kissed her lips. She felt she was floating on air.

"Poor kid. Feel better now?"

Kitty rested her head on his shoulder when he slid his long, muscular arm around her. She moved blissfully into the curve of his warm body.

Nate held her hand. "Darling, you know I love you," he murmured. "Let's quit kidding ourselves. I want you more than anything. We can be happy together. Don't you see?"

"Nate, you're so sweet, so giving, but . . ."

"I'm more than sweet and giving, Kitty, I'm in love with you." His lips found hers, stifling the protest she was about to make.

The telephone rang. He looked at her, uncertain.

"Ignore it," she whispered, trembling. "They'll leave a message."

But he couldn't do it. Sighing heavily, he rose and grabbed the receiver off the end of a table. "Yeah. This better be good." He paused. "Be right there."

"Sorry, hon. Got an emergency on my hands. I'll have to take you home." He glanced at the bedroom again and grumbled as she got up.

After Nate brought Kitty home, she fought sleep for a long time, wondering and fearing if he might be in danger. Then she finally nodded off.

It was nearly time to leave for the shop when the alarm rang. She thought of Nate as she hurriedly got dressed. Could they go on as they were doing? She doubted that. Nate wouldn't stand for it. He wanted marriage.

Kitty could already hear her mother's and Olivia's advice. They would both nod wisely and say, "If you love Nate, Kitty, dear, then marry him, by all means. Time is too precious to waste."

Easy for them to say, but it didn't help her conflicted sensibilities. At that moment she felt helpless. *Love makes us so vulnerable,* she thought sadly.

Chapter Fourteen

Nate came by the shop near closing time the next day, his broad shoulders straight. Her heart skipped a beat when she saw him stride through the door. For the moment, there were no customers and she was glad, because he tilted her head and kissed her softly.

"You look absolutely gorgeous," he said.

"You too." Her arms flew around his neck and his lips smothered hers with another insistent kiss.

He let her go and stood with his hands holding her wrists at arm's length, his eyes devouring her.

"I've missed you," she said with heartfelt fervor.

He grinned. "Since last night?"

"It seems longer than that. I was worried about you." Then, with that closed look on his face, she wished she could bite back the comment.

But he let it go. "I missed you, too, kid."

Kitty hugged him tight. He covered her throat and

earlobes with a tantalizing barrage of kisses, like a playful puppy.

Without warning, Nate's beeper went off. "Always at the wrong time!"

Kitty stepped back. He punched the cellular phone on, his face glowering. "Okay! Cut to the chase," he said to someone on the other end, waited a dozen seconds, then slammed the off button. "Got to run, darling. Something big's going down."

With a surge that could only be exhilaration, he kissed her hard, and ran out of the shop.

When Nate was gone, Kitty stood there, quaking with a sudden cold fear. He had never told her much about his profession: the criminals, the times he spent in surveillances, the arrests, the danger involved. But she knew these things went on. Did she have the stamina to be a policeman's wife like those women at the beach party—her own mother?

Nate called that night and they talked, but Kitty couldn't overcome her worry about him. It somehow stood between them, and their conversation became stilted. She wanted to ask him about the case he'd been on but knew he wouldn't tell her. They said good night.

Kitty came home from work the following evening. She brought Chinese food from one of her favorite takeout restaurants. She and Olivia sat down at the kitchen table and ate, first trying chopsticks, then laughing and giving up. With the last morsel finished, Kitty gathered the little cartons and threw them away.

"Why don't you join me in the library for coffee?" Olivia said. "It's almost time for 'Diagnosis Murder.' "

"Let me take a shower first, then I'll be right down."

Kitty hurried upstairs, pulling off her clothes as she went along, and slung them over her shoulder. By the time she reached the bathroom she was nearly naked. She turned on the shower faucet, adjusted the temperature, then got in, letting the hot water wash over her body. It had a soothing effect. Remembering her promise to Olivia, she made it a quick one and turned off the faucet, dried herself, and slipping into jeans and a big white shirt.

When she was about to go downstairs, the telephone rang. She sat down on the side of the bed and picked up the receiver, hoping it was Nate checking in.

"Kitty? Eric. Something awful's happened. I know Nate would want me to call. He's in the hospital—the one near the department. Can you come?"

"Oh, no! I'm on my way." Shocked, Kitty didn't ask him to explain but hung up and flew down the stairs to the library to tell Olivia.

"I can't watch television after all. Eric, Nate's friend, called. It's an emergency. Something happened to Nate."

Olivia's palms went to her cheeks, her color draining. "Oh, dear!"

Kitty ran to the garage, and in a matter of a few seconds, gunned out of the driveway. She felt cold sweat pop out on her forehead as she flogged the BMW into action, spurring the old car down the street as though Satan was on her tail. Hectic rush-hour traffic made driving slow. Her mind conjured up all sorts of grim scenes while she wove in and around other vehicles. Was Nate in an accident? Did his appendix rupture? *Please, don't let him be shot like my father!* She prayed. Crying out, she squeezed the steering wheel until her knuckles turned white, then she beat on it.

Her prayers became hymns of pure desperation. She felt like she was walking through a storm, terrified of not finding the light. Eric indicated it was bad. Why hadn't she asked him just how bad?

Nate got home from work and took his dog Awesome jogging. He needed a workout to clear his mind. He traveled further along the swamp than he usually ran. A prickling sensation on the back of his neck left him feeling as though someone were watching him. He slowed and looked around. The dog barked a warning. Sure enough, an alligator lay not more than thirty feet away, its opaque eyes following him. He gave it a wide berth and took another trail leading away from it. He glanced back over his shoulder just in case the darn thing got the bright idea to track him. But it lost interest.

The trail brought Nate closer to the water again. Another alligator was lying half submerged, sunning itself, its mouth open. A bird pecked at its teeth. He had read somewhere that birds clean an alligator's teeth after it eats but the story seemed farfetched to him. He half expected those massive jaws to chomp down.

Up ahead, he spotted two young boys playing in the shallows. Since this was alligator territory, they shouldn't be there. He jogged forward to tell them to climb out. Nate knew alligators didn't usually attack humans, but the boys' free-for-all could attract attention. And there had been incidents in the past.

Sure enough, a six-foot alligator lay among the reeds beside the water. Its mouth opened, displaying sharp pearlies, and it swished its tail. Then the beast clamped its teeth and swam into the swamp, submerging.

Nate yelled, " 'Gator! Get out of the water!"

They stopped their play and looked at him, unresponsive. It occurred to him that perhaps they didn't understand English. Nate commanded his dog to sit, then raced to the water and plunged in. The dog barked furiously from the grassy bank.

He never knew whether the alligator would have attacked the children, but in his effort to drive it away, he got into a tussle with the scaly thing. Taking him by the shoulder, it held him under the water.

When Kitty reached the hospital, she jumped out without locking the car, raced inside, and found Eric in the waiting room, his face ashen.

"Where is he?" she demanded. "What happened to Nate? Can I see him?"

"Sit down and I'll explain as best as I can," he said heavily.

Kitty perched on the edge of a chair, her eyes glued to Eric. She could tell by the dreadful look on his face that things were bad.

"First, he'll pull through." He heaved a sigh of relief.

Kitty felt like she was going to throw up and willed herself to get a grip.

"Go on, Eric. What happened? He was shot?"

"No. An alligator grabbed him and held him under. He nearly drowned."

"A what?"

"A 'gator. From what I heard, it bit his shoulder

and the doc had to take a lot of stitches. Lost a ton of blood. I guess the thing almost drowned him."

"This is unbelievable."

"You see, he was out jogging. Saw a couple of kids wading, and an alligator started swimming toward them. What could he do? He jumped in—tried to protect the kids."

His words blasted in her ears like torpedoes hitting their mark. "No!" she shouted. "This is incredible!"

A doctor in a baggy green surgical suit came out and Eric rushed over to him. Kitty leaped out of the chair.

"How's Nate Mansfield?" she asked over Eric's shoulder, her throat nearly constricted.

The doctor gazed at the two of them. "Are you family members?" he asked.

"Sure. Sister and brother," Eric lied.

"Well, Lt. Mansfield's vital signs are good. But his recovery will take time. He's in ICU."

Kitty grabbed Eric and they hugged each other with joy.

"When can I see him?" Kitty demanded.

"Maybe tomorrow." The doctor took off his glasses and stuck them in the pocket of his coat.

"I'm not leaving here until I see him," she insisted, her voice firm.

"That's the best I can do." The doctor turned and walked down the corridor.

Kitty sat back down. She knew she was in for a long night. "Nate's got grit," she said to Eric. "He'll be okay." But she wished she was as sure as she sounded. "What about the kids?"

"They're fine. Ran home and got help."

He grabbed a magazine off the rack on the wall,

slumped into the chair beside her and spread out his clunky athletic shoes.

With a weary sigh, she leaned her head back, resigned to sleeping the night in the chair. She turned to Eric. "When you fear someone you love might die, you realize just how precious they are to you." Then she choked up.

"Sure," Eric said. He patted her on the arm. "Try to get some sleep."

"That's easy for you to say." She gave him a lopsided grin.

Waiting to see Nate was a painful time of reflection. Kitty longed to rush into his hospital room and tell him how much she loved him. How foolishly blind she had been. People could get killed just crossing the street or slipping in the bathtub.

The image of the peonies he had given her flashes before her, and she realized that life could be as fragile as a flower petal. She longed to put her arms around his waist and kiss his warm lips, to see his eyes shining on hers.

"Nate's the most honest and decent and brave man I know," she said to Eric.

"Yeah, you're right, Kitty."

"I've been a puddin'-headed idiot, like Laurie said." She took out a tissue and blew her nose. "Nate wants to marry me, you know, but I've been shying away from saying yes, fearing something would happen. How did I know his heroism would involve an alligator and not bullets."

Eric shifted his bulk in the chair. "He knows that."

When they let Kitty in to see Nate the next morning her knees wobbled, her hair was in disarray, and she didn't have any lipstick on. But at this point she didn't care about appearances. The room was overly warm. She stared across the floor at him, her throat knotting up so hard she could hardly get her breath. He looked helpless lying there. Dark shadows circled his blue eyes, and the imprint of an oxygen mask was still visible around his nose. A long tube was attached to his arm, dripping in life-giving fluids. Kitty ached to reach out to him. Instead, she stood there like a stick, clutching her purse, with a tight smile.

"Kitty," Nate said, wincing. "Is this a bummer or what?"

She nodded and moistened her lips. "Yeah. You okay now?"

"Sure, babe."

She found her feet and rushed to his side to kiss him, careful not to disturb the needle. A scratch ran across his forehead. His other arm was bandaged. It made her wince.

"That was a nice brotherly kiss," he said. "How about a real Kitty-type kiss? You know, the kind that sends me to Jupiter and back."

His words made her chuckle and she felt a little better. Bending low, she kissed him thoroughly. Eric, who stood behind her slack-jawed, suddenly grinned.

"I know when I'm not wanted," he said. "Take care of yourself, good buddy."

"Thanks for waiting with me," Kitty told him.

Nate tried to raise himself but laid back down. "Come back later, Eric." Eric waved and scooted out.

"Darn it!" Nate said. "Here I get you alone and I can't even hug you. But why don't you climb up here and lie down with me? You're hovering there like my mother." His eyes flickered with mischief.

Kitty giggled, her heart filling with joy. "Now I know you're going to recover! But what if someone comes in?"

"So? They can go jump in the Atlantic."

Kitty pressed her lips together in disapproval, then he moved over very slowly. She lay down away from his injured shoulder, and slipped her arm under his head, meeting his loving eyes with a caress.

"So velvety," he murmured weakly, running his thumb over her lower lip. "I love your mouth. Did I ever tell you that?"

She shook her head and swallowed hard. "I've missed you, darling."

The corners of his lips turned up. "I like to hear you call me darling."

She squeezed his hand, and was about to kiss his cheek when she heard footsteps thumping down the hall. She jumped up and straightened her clothes. Those nurses!

The following day, friends and family trooped in and out, driving the hospital staff crazy.

Kitty sat beside his bed, holding his big hand. "This profusion of bouquets, with their colors and aromas, make your room look like a florist shop," she said.

He laughed. "Or a funeral parlor."

She turned on him. "Don't ever say that again, Nate!"

He shrugged his good shoulder. "It was meant to be funny."

"Well, it's not funny to me."

Mary arrived. Kitty embraced her. "Thanks for coming, Mom."

"I started out as soon as I got your call, Kitty."

Mary looked him over with a maternal eye and her face cracked into a smile. "Nate, you're too tough to drown. You'll be back on the job in no time."

Kitty could tell by his expression that it was just what he wanted to hear.

"I've been trying to tell your daughter that," he said, winking.

Olivia popped her head in the door. "Hello, everyone. Nate, dear, I brought you fresh roses from my garden." She beamed when Nate told her they were the most fragrant of all. Then she turned to Kitty, examining her. "You must eat something, Kit, dear," she chided good-naturedly. "Why don't you go down to the cafeteria and get a bite? We'll stay here and keep Nate company."

Kitty brushed aside the suggestion with a polite shake of the head. "I'll do that later."

Nate might appear to be recovering rapidly, but she could tell by his washed-out skin tone and the telltale grimaces he made, that he was putting on an act in order to reassure everyone he was fine. He'd lost a lot of blood.

The next afternoon, Kitty sat beside his bed reading to him from a joke book. He suddenly said in a serious voice, "When I was able to open my eyes after surgery, I thought I might be dead." He coughed, short and shallow, and grimaced. "Then my vision got better and the buzzing in my head settled down. What a relief. I'm not afraid of dying, mind you, but you wouldn't be there. I couldn't stand that." He cleared his throat and looked at her for a long time without speaking.

She felt like crying but held her emotions in check.

Then he added, "Until I got hurt, I never felt vulnerable. I just did the job I was trained to do. But as I lay here last night, the realization I'm not infallible hit me almost as hard as those big teeth."

"Oh, Nate, you will take care of yourself?" Kitty tried to hold back the tears, but for the first time, they tumbled down her cheeks like an avalanche.

In a few days, Nate left the hospital without his doctor's permission. Kitty was furious with him. He came by the shop and asked her to go to the policeman's ball the following Saturday.

Kitty took one look at him and said incredulously, "No! You ought to be in the hospital, Nate Mansfield! What are you thinking? If you won't take care of yourself, I refuse to go anywhere with you, let alone a ball. You're being ridiculous! You ought to be in bed."

"Then I'll take someone else!" he shot back.

Struck by his words, she lashed out, "Go ahead!" Then she fought back the sob that rose in her throat.

Kitty knew he needed to feel whole again, like a man, and that he was tired of being mothered, but she feared he'd relapse.

"Okay—I will!" He turned on his heel and headed for the door in a huff.

Kitty didn't attempt to deflect his bluster, but glared after him in pure frustration.

Chapter Fifteen

The clock hands on the wall pointed to a 6:45. Kitty emptied the till and closed the shop, dejected. An inner voice told her she could never marry Nate now and live with the uncertainty—the terrible, gnawing dread of his being killed.

After dinner, he came by. Olivia had gone to a movie with one of her bridge friends. He took the leather chair and Kitty sat down on the sofa. He looked troubled, his brows furrowed.

"I'm sorry I blew my top, Kitty."

She bit her lower lip and the tension drained out of her. "Oh, Nate, I was childish. I'm worried about your recovery, that's all."

He didn't speak for a moment. "I love you, darling, and I want you to marry me." He didn't wait for her reply but rushed on. "I'm prepared to give up police work, if that's what you want." He reached out to her, willing to give up his life's work for her.

182

Taken by surprise, she stammered, "You . . . you'd give up your career?" She could hardly comprehend what she was hearing.

"That's what I said."

"You know I can't let you do that. You're career has always come first."

His face took on a resolute set. "Not any more—not before you. I don't want to lose you. If that's what it will take, then that's what it takes."

Misery settled in the pit of her stomach. "But I can't take that responsibility. Oh, darn! You'd grow to hate me in time—I just know it."

He came and sat beside her, taking her hands. "Be reasonable. I'm willing to throw it all away for you because I love you. You're the most important thing in my life. Surely you must know that."

"Oh, gee! This is awful."

"Awful? I thought this was the very thing you wanted. You were opposed to my police work from the beginning, right? Make up your mind, woman."

"You've put me on the spot."

He looked at her wearily. "How?"

"Blackmail! That's what it is."

"Blackmail? Am I hearing you correct? You're not making sense."

"Go on, make a snide remark. But you'd be squirming out of your jeans in no time if you had to sit at a desk all day."

"Darling, let's not fight. I love you and need you desperately. What do you want me to say? I'm willing to give up the force because you come first. Is that wrong?"

"I feel like I'm flying apart inside. Nate, I . . ."

Nate softened his tone. "You won't marry me if I

stay on the force. And you won't marry me if I quit? I don't understand, babe."

"Don't you?" She fought to control her emotions. "I'm sorry. I can't let you give up what you love doing. I'm shocked—that's all. Oh, this is so unbelievable—you not being a cop."

He hesitated a moment, giving her a bleak stare. "What are you willing to give up for me, Kitty O'Hara?"

His question took the wind out of her sails. She twisted her hands, trying to think. Then it hit her, and she gave him a broad smile.

"Darling, I see it all now. It just popped into my head like that." She tapped her head. "I won't let you quit the force. Absolutely not. You asked me what I was willing to give up. Then it came to me, your willingness making it so clearly. Well, I'm willing to give up my fear." She laughed, thinking it was so obvious he couldn't help but see her meaning.

"Your fear?"

"I've been holding on to it like it was the Hope Diamond. That's what held me back—my inner fears. Oh, Nate, I know it's something I'll have to work on, but I'm willing to try. Your happiness is equally important to me, and your self-denial has taught me a lesson I'll never forget. I need you, too. Amazing, don't you think?"

"Amazing! Astounding! Wonderful!" Nate pulled her into his arms and tried not to wince from the pain in his shoulder. He couldn't believe his good fortune.

"I can have you and still stay on the force! Wow! Now I understand why you've shied away every time I mentioned marriage, even though, down deep, I knew." His face broadened into a grin.

She kissed him firmly. He laughed.

"What's so amusing?" she asked.

"The funny little way you tilt your head."

"Oh? What else?"

"Your adorable nose."

She chuckled. "Flattery will get you everywhere. Oh, darling, you can be proud, arrogant, impatient, disdainful, and driven, but I love you."

"How about warm, sympathetic, loving, and loyal?"

Her heart swelled. "All those things, too."

He leaned closer, his eyes intent. "Marry me tonight."

She stiffened. "What? You just got out of the hospital!"

"I dare you."

"But . . ."

"You always took a dare when we were kids. Why not now? We'll fly to Las Vegas. I know a guy who runs a charter service."

"Be serious."

She hadn't said no, and he could tell by the look in her eyes she considered his offer.

"I want you, darling. Why wait any longer? Haven't we done enough of that already?" he said.

He kissed her long and hard until she broke free, gasping.

"You've convinced me. Call your pilot friend. I'm going to dash upstairs and throw a few things in my suitcase." She danced around. "I can't believe I'm actually doing this." She looked about the room, almost frantic but laughing. "Don't let me forget to leave messages for Mom and Olivia. And what dress should I take along?"

Nate chuckled and picked up the telephone. "You'll have to decide on that one, babe."